Praise for Deb Kastner

"Kastner's latest will grab the reader with familiar characters and engaging dialogue."
—*RT Book Reviews* on *Yuletide Baby*

"In this endearing final installment of the E-mail Order Brides series, Kastner provides an original twist on the 'alter egos' storyline, and her characters' struggles with identity are relatable."
—*RT Book Reviews* on *Meeting Mr. Right*

"A wonderful story about sharing burdens, finding faith and discovering the life one dreams of may already be the one you have."
—*RT Book Reviews* on *A Colorado Match*

Praise for Arlene James

"The charms of small-town life and the community's spirit blossoms in this Heart of Main Street series opener."
—*RT Book Reviews* on *Love in Bloom*

"Kendra and Jack realistically struggle to overcome hardships and learn to love in this compelling continuation of the Texas Twins miniseries."
—*RT Book Reviews* on *Carbon Copy Cowboy*

"Warm, rich details combine with Southern charm and hospitality in this touching story about healing deep emotional wounds with God's help."
—*RT Book Reviews* on *Second Chance Match*

Award-winning author **Deb Kastner** lives and writes in beautiful Colorado. Since her daughters have grown into adulthood and her nest is almost empty, she is excited to be able to discover new adventures, challenges and blessings, the biggest of which is her sweet grandchildren. She enjoys reading, watching movies, listening to music, singing in the church choir and attending concerts and musicals.

Arlene James has been publishing steadily for nearly four decades and is a charter member of RWA. She is married to an acclaimed artist, and together they have traveled extensively. After growing up in Oklahoma, Arlene lived thirty-four years in Texas and now abides in beautiful northwest Arkansas near two of the world's three loveliest, smartest, most talented granddaughters. She is heavily involved in her family, church and community.

Yuletide Cowboys

Deb Kastner

&

Arlene James

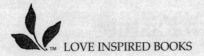 LOVE INSPIRED BOOKS

Recycling programs for this product may not exist in your area.

ISBN-13: 978-0-373-87994-6

Yuletide Cowboys

Copyright © 2015 by Harlequin Books S.A.

The publisher acknowledges the copyright holders of the individual works as follows:

The Cowboy's Yuletide Reunion
Copyright © 2015 by Debra Kastner

The Cowboy's Christmas Gift
Copyright © 2015 by Deborah Rather

www.Harlequin.com

Printed in U.S.A.

CONTENTS

THE COWBOY'S
YULETIDE REUNION

Deb Kastner

To my family. You manage to live with me despite crazy tight deadlines, a messy house and endless fast food. Love you all!

Then the angel said to them,
"Do not be afraid, for I bring you tidings of great joy
Which will be to all people.
For there is born to you this day in the city of David
A Savior, who is Christ the Lord."
—*Luke* 2:10–11

Chapter One

❧

"Cowabunga!" Marcus Ender stomped on the brake of his truck and jerked the steering wheel to the right, nearly jackknifing the empty horse trailer he was towing behind him. Snow glistened on the evergreen branches and banked along the sides of the road where the plow had gone through.

At first he thought he was seeing things. But no.

The animal was there right in front of his eyes, all right—except it wasn't a cow that had bounded into the road and completely blocked his truck from passing. Marcus narrowed his gaze on the antlered beast.

Not an elk. Not a deer—at least not the white-tailed variety that one generally expected to find in the thickly forested Colorado landscape. He rubbed his eyes with the palms of his hands.

A *reindeer*? Like the kind that pulled Santa's sleigh? Up on the housetop and all that?

Man, was this thing lost. Like on another continent, lost—or wherever the North Pole was supposed to be. Geography had never been Marcus's best subject.

He chuckled. The reindeer, which stood right in front

of his truck with garland draped around its neck, calmly ruminated and stared back at him as if *he* were the odd man out.

Maybe he was. Texas born and raised in Oklahoma, he had never been to Colorado before. He wouldn't be here now if he wasn't doing a favor for his Grandma Sheryl. He was already anticipating being home for the holidays at his grandmother's ranch in Red Bluff, Oklahoma. His older brother, Matt, had already arrived, celebrating the holiday with the family for his first time in years. Marcus didn't know how he felt about that—he and Matt had never gotten along well and hadn't seen each other in a long time, but he hadn't been the one to put distance between them, and he wasn't about to let Matt ruin the holidays for him.

He'd just pick up the horses here that his grandmother had purchased and be on his way—as soon as the reindeer decided to move. It was taking its own good time about it.

He was about to roll down the window and shake his hat at it, but then it occurred to him that the animal must belong to someone, probably a local, if the garland was anything to go by. Could reindeer be domesticated? He had no idea how much one cost, but he was guessing they couldn't be cheap.

It wasn't in his nature to drive away when he might be able to help someone find a missing pet, and anyway, he was curious. He hoped it was tame.

Did reindeer bite? Worse yet, since he didn't know what he was doing with a live reindeer, he ran the distinct prospect of antlers prodding his hindquarters.

Taking a deep breath and whispering a prayer for safety, he gently opened the cab door, half expecting the reindeer to dart away into the brush, or worse yet, charge *him*. It lifted its head and followed his movements but didn't appear to be startled by his presence.

"Easy now," he murmured gently. He took one step toward it, then two. "We're all friends here, right?"

The reindeer's ears twitched forward as if it understood what he was saying.

"Right," he repeated, verbally reassuring himself. As a general rule he liked animals and they responded in kind, but a reindeer?

Even if he could get next to it and even if it was somehow tagged with an address—which was highly unlikely, now that he thought about it—what was he going to do with it? Sure, he was pulling a horse trailer, but there was no way he would attempt to load a wild animal into it.

He heard the clip-clop of a horse's hooves on the pavement behind him and turned just in time to see a woman riding bareback toward him on a very large black draft horse. The sun shone directly behind her and Marcus lowered his straw cowboy hat over his brow to shade his eyes. He couldn't make out more than her shadow, but she looked downright diminutive on top of the enormous Percheron.

"I see you've met Crash," she said with a spritely laugh.

Marcus froze at the sound of her voice, and for a moment he thought his heart stopped beating.

He knew that voice. He knew that *laugh*.

"Sarah?"

"Marcus?" Sarah sounded just as stunned as he felt, as well she should be. What was his high school sweetheart doing out here in the middle of the Colorado forest?

Even if he hadn't recognized her voice, his heart affirmed the truth and his pulse raced wildly at the thought of seeing her again. It had been a long time. As far as Marcus was concerned, too long. Either that, or not nearly long enough.

Sarah trotted up to him and reined the horse to a halt. He reached for the horse's head without a second thought. She'd been riding with nothing more than a rope halter to guide her enormous mount.

He wasn't surprised that Sarah rode with such ease. She'd always had a way with horses.

And reindeer, apparently. Crash, was it?

"I don't understand," she said, effortlessly swinging her leg around and sliding off the Percheron. She looked thinner than he remembered her, and the circles under her eyes were almost as dark as her sable hair, which she had pulled back into a loose ponytail. She'd slung a lariat across her shoulder and looked halfway as if she'd just ridden out of an old Western. "What are you doing here?"

Without taking the time to think through his actions, Marcus grinned and enveloped her in an impromptu hug. He'd always respected the value of a good hug, even before spending the past several years working as a counselor at a ranch for troubled teens. To his dismay, she immediately stiffened in his embrace. He dropped his arms and stepped back, feeling as awkward as the youth he was when he'd seen her last. He cleared his throat, wondering what to say to break the silence.

"I suppose I could ask the same thing of you." Marcus paused and then clicked his tongue as the realization sprung on him. "Except I think I already know."

Grandma Sheryl had sent him on this errand to

pick up some horses she'd bought on his way to her Oklahoma ranch, and he'd agreed without even remotely suspecting an alternate motive. Anything for his grandma—anything except this. Grandma wasn't usually so sly. Heat rushed to his face and he lowered his head so Sarah wouldn't see his flaming cheeks.

Why hadn't it occurred to him before that Grandma Sheryl might have something up her sleeve? He wouldn't put it past her to have cooked up some nutty matchmaking scheme. How was he going to explain *that* to Sarah? Her reception could be termed less than enthusiastic.

"I didn't expect...*you*," Sarah admitted, voicing exactly what Marcus had been thinking. "When I spoke to your grandmother, I had the impression she was sending one of her wranglers to collect my horses from me, not one of her grandsons."

"If it makes any difference, she didn't tell me I'd be seeing you, either."

"Oh."

That one syllable pretty much summed it up. His skin prickled as if he was breaking out in hives. Had it not occurred to Grandma Sheryl that this encounter might not go well? That Sarah might not want to see him again? He and Sarah hadn't parted on the best of terms after they'd graduated from high school, and they hadn't seen each other since. And she didn't sound as if she was too thrilled about the prospect of seeing him now.

"I'm just here to collect the horses and then I'll get out of your hair," he promised, grinning despite the discomfort of his churning stomach.

"Fine," she agreed with a clipped nod. She wasn't even trying to smile. "But first I need to take care of Crash. Clever girl somehow opened the paddock gate and decided to take a little hike on her own. I was afraid I might have lost her for good."

Marcus eyed Crash and then the Percheron. "How do you plan to get her back to your ranch?"

She chuckled, but to his keen ears it sounded forced. He laughed along with her, hoping that would encourage her not to stress over it. Chasing a runaway reindeer was kind of funny in a way, but maybe not if you were the owner of said reindeer.

"It's a Christmas tree farm, not a ranch. And I've brought my trusty lariat along to catch the errant reindeer," she said, tilting her head to look up at him, the sudden sparkle in her gray eyes making Marcus's breath catch in his throat. "Can you give me a boost? Mag here is as gentle as a lamb but he's a big ol' brute."

"I'll say," Marcus agreed, threading his fingers to provide a hand-made stirrup. She steadied herself by gripping his shoulder and their gazes met and held for what seemed like an eternity, but which was probably only a few seconds, long enough for electricity to zing through him and rev his pulse.

They were both older now, and hopefully wiser, but apparently some things never changed, such as the way her gray eyes could so easily capture his and jolt him right down to his core. Such as the way his head spun when he inhaled the sweet apple of her shampoo, the same scent she'd worn when they were dating in high school.

What would Grandma Sheryl think of that?

Better for him if she didn't find out. He swallowed hard and boosted Sarah up onto Mag's sturdy back, half-relieved when she was no longer in his arms, and yet he felt oddly vacant.

"Is Mag short for something?" he asked, trying to turn his mind to something less hazardous.

"Magnificent. The other half of his team is Jes— Majestic."

"Clever. And accurate."

"Thank you. I named them myself." She seemed to sit a little taller as she slipped the lariat off her shoulder and nudged Mag forward with her heels. To Marcus's surprise, Crash didn't budge when the large draft horse trotted in her direction, and Sarah easily slid the loop over the reindeer's neck.

"Okay, now, Crash, let's get you back home where you belong." She glanced behind her to Marcus, leaning her free hand on Mag's flanks. "You can follow me back to the farm in your truck."

"That won't bother the animals?"

"Not if you don't tailgate."

She flashed him a cheeky grin, turned forward and kicked Mag into a quick trot. Crash snuffed in protest but held back for only a moment before following her without any more hesitation. Marcus couldn't say that he blamed the reindeer.

There was a time when he would have followed Sarah anywhere.

Sarah couldn't seem to catch a breath nor calm her erratic pulse. She was painfully aware of the deep purr of Marcus's truck directly behind her, but she didn't dare glance backward to see if he was following at a safe distance.

He was. He was Marcus, after all.

Marcus Ender. He'd been on her mind often in recent weeks, but she'd never considered that she might actually see him again. He was her happy place, the spot in her mind and the high point of her past memories where she went when she needed to remember the way things used to be, when in her innocence and naïveté she'd believed the whole wonderful world stretched before her, full of adventures and blessings. Before she'd grown up and finally understood how painful life really was.

To her deep regret, little had gone right in her life since she'd graduated from high school and left small-town Oklahoma behind for the thrill of Colorado. She'd been full of ideals and intentions, the promise of higher education and making it out on her own.

She'd graduated college, but then her life had gone off on a tangent she never would have expected. Things had gotten bad. Then worse. Then downright terrible. Right now she felt as if she was drowning. She would have long since given up trying to succeed at all if it weren't for her beloved daughters. Even given all the misfortunes she'd encountered, she would do it all again in a heartbeat for Onyx and Jewel.

Every day, with every ounce of her being, she fought for her children and prayed for them and worked for things to get better. But they didn't get better, and no matter how hard she prayed, the Lord didn't appear to answer her, or even hear her meager pleas. Lately she'd stopped asking.

Crash snuffed, bringing her abruptly back to the present. The reindeer pulled back unexpectedly, contending with the rope around her neck. The lariat tightened and nearly slipped from Sarah's fingers. She dropped the horse's reins and grabbed the rope with both hands, tugging against the stubborn reindeer. That's all she needed, to have Crash bolt and run. This day was already a prime disaster in the making without silly reindeer games.

She snorted at her unintentional pun. Oh, she was funny today. And it was only going to get better from here.

Marcus had come to take away the last vestiges of her life with her late husband, Justin. Mag and Jes, the Percheron team that had once drawn the sleigh taking cheery guests out into the woods to find the perfect Christmas tree, would now be part of Sheryl Ender's breeding program—or something. They hadn't really discussed why Sheryl wanted to purchase the draft horses from her. Last she knew, the older lady and her business partner bred and trained quarter horses for barrel racing. Percherons seemed a far cry from that, but if Sheryl had use for the Percherons and would give a good price for them, who was Sarah to complain?

At least her beloved horses were going to someone she trusted and admired. Tears pricked the corner of her eyes, but she dashed them away with the back of her hand.

No more tears. She was done crying.

The only animals left at the farm after the Percherons departed would be Snort and Crash. She had no idea what she was going to do with a couple of live reindeer. Trying to sell them a week before Christmas was like trying to pawn penny candy at a gourmet chocolate shop. An added stress to an already bleak season.

The sky, which only minutes before had been a pale blue and lined with a few fluffy clouds on the horizon, had now turned a dark, ominous mixture of colors as a storm surged over the front range of the Rocky Mountains. Sarah was familiar with Colorado weather and how abruptly things could change. Some days you could get a tan in the morning and build a snowman by midafternoon. She sensed the change as much as saw it, breathed the feeling of imminent snow in the air, and moments later large white flakes were spitting from the sky.

She glanced back at Marcus. He was following close enough that she could see the half smile on his lips, but his expressive eyes were shadowed by the brim of his hat. He'd appeared every bit as shocked as she was at their unexpected encounter with each other, and she wondered what he thought about it now.

She shook her head and scoffed at herself. Why did it matter? He would load the Percherons in his trailer and be on his way within the hour. That would be the best thing for both of them, if he left without lingering. The less time they had to spend together, the better.

Unfortunately, her plan to be quickly rid of Marcus hinged on the weather, which wasn't cooperating at *all*. The sky was glowing a dark purplish-gray color. Not a good sign.

By the time they reached the farm several minutes later, the ground was already covered with a fresh blanket of snow and there was no end in sight. The already snow-packed roads would be extra slick, with dangerous patches of black ice lurking just under the white blanket. Marcus's truck was a four-wheel drive, but she doubted that would help him navigate the difficult landscape, especially with a trailer attached. Winter driving was tricky for those experienced with the conditions. She didn't know where Marcus had been in the past twelve years, but if he still lived in Oklahoma, he wouldn't be familiar with the ferocity of this weather.

Reaching the barn, she threw her leg across Mag's

flank and jumped to the ground, then set her heels and tugged on Crash's rope, urging her toward the barn. One would have thought the errant reindeer would be easily tempted by the prospect of warmth and food, but apparently not. The crazy animal planted her four hooves and straightened her neck and pulled her entire weight backward.

Stubborn, stubborn reindeer.

She was still mumbling a few choice words about fur rugs and venison steaks when Marcus exited his truck. He chuckled. "Need a hand?"

Sarah's first instinct was to refuse. She didn't need Marcus's help with anything. But then common sense took over and she tossed him the rope. It wasn't his fault she was mad at the world and everything in it.

"Knock yourself out."

"Well, I hope not, darlin'. It'll take more than one feisty reindeer to sweep me off my feet." He winked at her and her treacherous heart fluttered.

Marcus was six foot two and built like a brick wall, but it still took a great deal of tugging on his part to get the stubborn reindeer moving again. Sarah directed him to Crash's stall and then put up Mag, giving the Percheron a good rubdown and a bucket of oats to help tide him over for the long journey ahead.

Marcus could probably use a good pick-me-up as well, maybe a stout cup of coffee for the road, but Sarah hesitated to invite him up to the house.

For one thing, Onyx and Jewel and her parents-in-law, Carl and Eliza, were inside the cabin. There would be the obligatory introductions and Marcus, ever the social butterfly, would no doubt get caught up in the moment after finding himself accosted by the friendly elderly couple, the enthusiastic three-year-old and the unquestionably adorable baby.

Another reason she had qualms about bringing Marcus around had to do with the state of her house. It was in dire need of repair, from the missing tiles on the roof to a kitchen cabinet half falling off the hinges. Then there was the starkness of the decor, or rather, a lack of any sort of decor whatsoever. She'd pawned nearly every piece of furniture and all of the artwork to pay the most pressing of recent bills. There was only a smattering of pieces left—such as a beat-up old olive-green armchair and a hideaway sofa that had seen better days.

It would be obvious to even the most dispassionate of observers that she was in dire straits, and of all the people on planet earth, Marcus was the last man she'd want to have discover her this way. Her cheeks heated. Oh, the humiliation of it all.

The whole reason she'd broken up with him on the day after their high school graduation was so that she could go out and make a success of herself. They were headed in different directions and she couldn't be held back by a long-distance relationship. She needed to stay focused on her studies so she would never end up sending her kids to school wearing secondhand clothes as she'd had to do when she was a child. She was going to make something of herself.

Ha. What a joke that had turned out to be. She was dangling precariously by a thread right now, and it grew thinner all the time. But Marcus didn't need to know that—any of it. A woman had her pride, after all.

Marcus stood near the stable door, his hat in his hand and his brow drawn in an unusually solemn expression as he stared out at the landscape. She was about ready to suggest they load up the Percherons so he could be on his way when he turned to her and threaded his fingers through his thick golden hair.

"The weather has taken a turn for the worse." She knew he was trying his best to sound conversational, but she could hear the note of worry underlying his tone.

She stepped up beside him and peered out over the landscape, already knowing what she was going to see but still hoping beyond hope that he was overreacting.

He wasn't. His truck was already covered with a half inch of heavy snow. She couldn't even see the tracks the truck had made driving in. Perhaps worst of all, the wind was lashing the snow sideways, leaving zero visibility. She could barely make out the lights from the cabin, even though it was located only a few hundred yards from the stable.

"You're right. This doesn't look good," she agreed tightly, her throat going dry.

Oh no.

Her worst-case scenario was rapidly becoming her only option. What else was she to do?

Marcus frowned and settled his hat on his head. "No, it doesn't look good at all. I'd best load up the horses and head out of here before the storm gets any worse."

As much as she didn't want to do it, she laid a restraining hand on his arm. "I'm afraid we're too late for that. It looks like you're going to have to take your hat off and stay awhile.

Chapter Two

Was it his imagination or had Sarah's shoulders slumped when she'd suggested they go up to her house? Did his presence bother her that much?

It was a disheartening notion, but she was right about one thing—he wasn't going anywhere, at least not for a few hours yet. He'd never seen anything like this sudden turn in the weather. The already snow-packed roads were receiving a double wallop of the white stuff. Snow on snow. He didn't even want to think about trying to drive in it, especially towing a trailer with Grandma Sheryl's precious equine cargo. Odd, though, that he hadn't seen any quarter horses. Only the two Percherons, and Grandma wouldn't have any use for those.

For the moment a steaming-hot cup of black coffee and the opportunity to catch up with Sarah sounded great to him, even if she didn't appear equally enthused.

As they approached the house, Marcus darted around her to get the door, but it opened before he could get his hand around the knob, nearly sending him careening into the cabin.

Startled, Marcus stepped back. A white-haired old

man with a bushy beard greeted them and hastily ushered them inside. The guy was a dead ringer for Santa, from the rosy cheeks and the glitter in his eyes to his round belly. The only thing missing from the picture was a bow-like smile, which had been replaced by a worried frown. No bowl-full-of-jelly laughter here.

The fellow fit right into the surroundings, seeing as this was a Christmas tree farm and all. But what was he doing in her cabin? Sarah retained her very own Santa Claus and the man lived in her house?

"Thank the good Lord you're safely home," the man exclaimed in a booming bass voice. "Eliza is in a tizzy. She was just about ready to send me out after you in this blizzard. I'm grateful you came back when ya did. I wouldn't want to have had to chase ya through the snow."

"Sorry, Pops." Sarah brushed the white flakes from her dark hair and removed her snow boots and down jacket. "Pops, this is Marcus, one of Sheryl Ender's grandsons. He's here to pick up the horses, but unfortunately, the storm waylaid him. Marcus, this is my father-in-law, Carl Kendricks."

"Good to meet you, sir," Marcus replied automatically, shaking the older man's hand. He was glad he didn't have to think about the effort because his mind was busy wrapping itself around what he'd just learned.

Sarah was married. There was no reason why she shouldn't be. She was a beautiful woman with a heart of gold. He didn't know why the news came as a surprise to him, except that—

He glanced at her left ring finger, but it was bare.

Divorced, maybe? But then why would she be living with her husband's parents?

"Sarah?" a woman called from the next room. "Is that

you, honey? We were starting to get worried what with the snow croppin' up and all. Jewel just woke up from her nap. I fed her a bottle but she's still fussy. I think she wants her mama."

A pleasantly plump white-haired woman—Mrs. Claus, if Marcus didn't miss his guess—bustled into the room with a baby on one hip and a young dark-haired girl following along, hiding behind her grandmother's leg. The children were beautiful, the spitting images of their mother.

"Oh," the older woman exclaimed when she saw Marcus. "I didn't realize you had company."

Marcus grinned. "I'm here for the horses."

"One of Sheryl's grandsons," Carl supplied. "Marcus, this is my wife, Eliza."

"You're from Oklahoma? Did you go to school with Sarah?"

Marcus's gaze shifted to Sarah. Went to school with her? He'd *dated* her, for all four years of high school. He'd thought they were headed for an engagement and a wedding.

How wrong could a man be?

"I—er—yes, ma'am. We were in the same class together." He figured it was best to stick with the broad picture. No sense bringing up the past when her husband might waltz into the room at any moment.

Awkward.

"You all settle in now. Marcus, go ahead and shuck your coat and boots at the door," Eliza said, handing the baby to Sarah. "Coffee's already on. I'll grab an extra cup. I figured you'd need something to warm your innards after being out in that mess. Storm's a brewin'." She gestured toward the front window. Outside the wind swirled the large snowflakes both horizontally and vertically, creating a virtual whiteout. "Did you find Crash?"

"Silly reindeer was a good mile or so away, standing right in the middle of the road and blocking Marcus's truck."

"She wouldn't budge," Marcus added with a chuckle, winking at Eliza. "Good thing for me that Sarah happened along. I've never been face-to-face with a real live reindeer before. I didn't know what to do with her."

"Crash would have moved eventually, when she got hungry enough," Sarah said.

Marcus switched his gaze to her. There was something—*off*—in her tone, and even holding her baby, she had her arms wrapped around herself in a universally defensive gesture. He couldn't put his finger on it, but his years as a counselor had given him a sixth sense where people's emotions were concerned, even when they were trying to hide them.

Sarah was trying to conceal her feelings but she still sounded…down. Maybe even depressed.

His chest ached. His heart hurt for her, even if he didn't know why. She seemed as if she had it all—a beautiful family, a Christmas tree farm. Even live reindeer. How cool was that?

A thought hit him like a punch to the gut. Was *he* the reason she was sad?

"I've been meaning to ask—what is Sheryl going to do with a couple of Percherons, anyway?" Carl queried, running a hand down the gristle on his face.

Marcus didn't know whether to answer the question or ask two more. How did Carl and Eliza know Grandma Sheryl? And more to the point, what was this about him being here to take the Percherons?

"Wait—what? I'm not here for barrel racers? Quarter horses?"

"*Quarter* horses?" Eliza snorted. "In case you haven't noticed, we're not running a ranch here, son. What would a Christmas tree farm be doing with rodeo stock?"

Marcus didn't have a clue what a Christmas tree farm would do with barrel racers, but he was equally stymied as to why Grandma Sheryl, who trained quarter horses for rodeo would buy a couple of Percherons. It didn't make any sense.

"We use the drafts to pull the sleigh," Eliza continued.

"Used," Sarah corrected dully.

Now Marcus *knew* something was wrong, and unless he was the one causing the problem, he didn't want to leave until he'd uncovered the reason for her misery and discovered a way he could make her smile again.

Unfortunately, that was out of his hands. He was here to pick up the horses and go—as soon as the snow let up.

Sarah slouched into a shabby olive-green armchair and shifted the baby to her shoulder. She gestured to the little girl, who was still hiding behind Eliza's ample frame, one big dark eye peering out at him suspiciously.

It was going to take some work for him to win Sarah's trust when she obviously didn't want him here, but Marcus suspected he knew how to deal with the little one, who was a pint-size replica of her beautiful mother.

He crouched to the child's level and flashed his thousand-watt smile. He knew his strengths, and his grin topped the list, or so the ladies told him, both young and old. He hoped making friends with Sarah's daughter might be the first step in repairing his relationship with Sarah.

He reached out his hand to the preschooler. "Hey there, little lady. My name is Marcus. What's yours?"

He held his breath as he awaited her response. The moment stretched out indefinitely as the little girl stared at him, her lips in an adorable little pout. Second only to the first time he'd asked Sarah on a date, this was maybe the most important female he'd ever wanted to impress.

"I'm Onyx, and I'm three," she declared, holding up three fingers. She stepped out from behind her grandmother and reached for his hand, her expression as serious as her handshake. "That's my baby sister, Jewel, my mama is holding."

"Pleased to meet you, Onyx—and Jewel," he said, meeting her solemn tone with one equally as earnest. "I'm an old friend of your mama's."

"'Kay. Granny, can I go play with Buttons now?"

Marcus had never been *quite* so summarily dismissed by a female before. He turned to Sarah and arched a brow, grinning crookedly. "Buttons?"

"Her rabbit."

He'd been bested by a bunny.

Sarah couldn't believe how quickly Marcus pulled Onyx out of her shell. The little girl had been a precocious and outgoing toddler, but after the death of her father she'd become withdrawn and suspicious about everybody and everything. No matter what Sarah did to try to coax her into meeting people and trying new things, nothing seemed to work. All Marcus had to do was grin at her and the child immediately fell subject to his charm.

Sarah couldn't blame her. It was hard not to respond to Marcus's natural appeal, especially because he knew what he had and how to use it. The first time he'd turned that smile upon her she'd been a goner. Her heart fluttered at the memory. But that was a long time ago. Things were different now and she was well beyond the possibility of being flattered by a handsome face and charming smile.

Marcus moved to the front window, pressing his hands into the front pockets of his jeans. "I guess I'd better get going before the storm gets any worse."

"What? No. You can't go out in that!" Sarah's heart leaped into her throat as Marcus swiveled toward her, clearly surprised at her outburst. Her exclamation had been one of sheer panic. She'd practically shouted the words. Poor Jewel gave a distressed yelp and flailed her little arms in surprise.

Heat rushed to her face as he narrowed his gaze on her, silently studying her, his jaw tight and strain rippling across his broad shoulders.

"You can't leave *yet*," she amended, consciously leveling her voice even though her pulse was hammering. "It's not safe for you to drive in a whiteout, especially if you're not used to this kind of weather." She knew she still sounded flustered. How could she explain her irrational fear of snowstorms without going into personal details she'd rather avoid?

"It's really coming down out there. I can hardly see my truck from here. How long do you think before it stops? I'd hate to put you out any more than I have to. Maybe another hour or so?"

"An hour?" Sarah forced a chuckle and shook her head. "I'm afraid you're unfamiliar with Colorado blizzards. It'll be a day, maybe more, before this storm blows over."

His eyes widened and his jaw went slack. "A day?"

She nodded. "At the very least. I'm afraid you have no other option. You'll have to stay the night here as a guest in our home. I don't want to risk you putting yourself—or Mag and Jes—in danger." She paused and worried her bottom lip with her teeth. "Oh. I didn't ask about your family. Will your wife be worried about you?"

His eyes widened. "Wife? No—I'm not married. But I'd best call Grandma Sheryl and let her know there's been a delay. I don't want her to worry."

She didn't know why she breathed a sigh of relief when he said he was single. His marital status or the lack of was certainly no business of hers. But that didn't stop her traitorous heartbeat from quickening.

"I'll make up a guest room for you," she said to hide her sudden disorientation. She felt a little dizzy, as if the ground was rocking beneath her. "It's our spare room and we use it for storage, but there's a bed you can use for the night."

Marcus opened his mouth as if to protest, then glanced over his shoulder at the heavy snowfall and nodded. "I appreciate the offer. I hope I'm not putting you out too much."

"Not at all," Eliza inserted before Sarah could answer. "We're glad to have you. I'm sure you and Sarah will enjoy catching up with each other."

Enjoy wasn't exactly the word Sarah would have used. The last thing she wanted to do was share with Marcus all the trials she'd been through recently, but she had a feeling she was about to do just that. He'd always had a way of drawing her out when they were dating in high school.

"Will your husband be able to make it home through the storm, do you think?"

Sarah choked on her breath and Eliza audibly inhaled. Carl coughed to fill the sudden silence.

Marcus looked from one of them to another, his brow lowering over the bright blue of his eyes. "I'm sorry, did I say something wrong?"

"Justin passed away last year at Christmas," Sarah whispered over the lump in her throat.

"I'm so sorry. I didn't know."

"No. Of course you didn't."

"How about that coffee?" Eliza asked a little too brightly. She turned and bustled off into the kitchen.

Marcus threaded his fingers through his hair, ruffling the thick blond waves. He paced a few feet and then turned and strode back again, looking as uncomfortable as she'd ever seen him.

"Please sit down." She couldn't talk to him while he was pacing around like a caged tiger. "You're making me nervous."

He rubbed his palms down his thighs and gnawed at the inside of his cheek, eyeing the opposite end of the sofa from where Pops was sitting, but not moving to seat himself. The older man cleared his throat and stood.

"I think I'll check on Onyx," he said, his voice unusually scratchy. They didn't often talk about Justin, and Sarah was afraid the topic was upsetting him—just what he didn't need with his heart condition.

"Why don't you go lie down and rest for a bit?" she suggested.

He nodded. "Maybe I will."

Marcus waited until Carl had left the room before gingerly seating himself on the edge of the couch, his back ramrod straight as he leaned forward and clasped his hands between his knees. His gaze met hers, an outpouring of sympathy and curiosity.

Where did she even begin?

He smiled openly, encouraging her to speak without actually speaking. When he finally did say something, his words were the exact opposite of what she'd expected. "You don't have to talk about it if you'd rather not."

Suddenly the need to unburden herself flooded her chest and she was unable to stop herself. She'd carried this load alone for far too long. The farm and the girls kept her too busy to maintain close friendships with anyone in town, and she couldn't burden her in-laws with her doubts and fears. Marcus would be leaving as soon as the snow let up. What difference would it make if she shared some of the more difficult portions of her life with him? It wasn't as if she was going to see him again. And he always had been a good listener.

"No, I don't mind. I just don't want to upset Granny and Pops. Justin has been gone for a year now, but the loss is still tender for them."

He nodded. "I can imagine. For you and the children, as well."

She nodded and tried to swallow around the lump of emotion clogging her throat, blinking back the tears that burned in the corners of her eyes. She hadn't allowed herself to cry in months, and now already today she'd been on the verge of tears several times.

Eliza returned with steaming red-and-green-striped mugs of coffee, then excused herself and followed her husband down the hall. Sarah watched silently until she was out of sight.

"How'd you meet Justin?" Marcus asked.

That wasn't the question she'd expected and it took her off guard. Most people only wanted to know how he'd died, not how they'd met.

"In a marketing class my last year of college. He

was twelve years older than me and I thought the fact that his family owned a Christmas tree farm was romantic." She laughed drily at the irony. She and Justin had had a happy marriage, but nothing over-the-moon and starry-eyed. Not as she'd felt when she was with Marcus. "We dated for a little over a year and then he asked me to marry him."

Marcus's smile looked strained. She couldn't blame him. It was an odd conversation to be having with an ex. "You said yes, obviously."

"It seemed like the next logical step."

His eyebrows rose. "Logical?"

She shrugged. "You know me. Ever the pragmatist."

"I remember. You told me not to bring you flowers so often because they faded and died within a week and my money could be better spent on other things."

"Which is true. As I recall, you never listened to me."

"That's because you deserve pretty things and I enjoyed giving them to you."

Her stomach fluttered when she realized he'd used the present tense of *deserve*, as if he still felt something for her. He'd always had the habit of saying things that ruffled her. Apparently that hadn't changed with time.

"The farm belongs to Justin's family. I moved out here and did computer coding work at home until Onyx came along. After that I dropped back to part-time so I could take care of her."

"And Jewel?"

"Jewel was born after Justin passed away. His accident was on Christmas Eve last year. I was three months pregnant at the time."

Marcus captured her gaze with his, his eyes clouding with sympathy and concern.

She didn't want him to feel sorry for her, especially since the story was only going to go downhill from here. She remembered how naturally empathetic and sensitive Marcus was, how he'd always seemed to be able to feel her emotions. He rode her roller coaster of highs and lows right along with her. The more she told him now the worse it would be. Her pride flared at the realization that he might pity her. She couldn't even stand to think about that.

Her current position wasn't entirely her fault. Most of the blame lay at Justin's feet. But she owned up to her own role in the drama.

A deep, undecipherable sound echoed from his throat. He reached for her but she instinctively jerked back. If Marcus put his arms around her right now she would lose it, and she refused to cry in front of him.

He lowered his arms, his hands twitching into fists. The corners of his full lips bowed downward, and her stomach churned. She hadn't meant to hurt his feelings, but she had only a tenuous hold on her own emotions and she simply couldn't risk it.

"There was an unexpected storm on the day before Christmas last year—much like this one. It came out of nowhere and created whiteout conditions on the roads.

"Onyx had seen a television commercial for this specific doll and it was all she talked about for a good month solid. Naturally it was the top-selling girl's toy that year. We'd planned to do our shopping on Black Friday but no matter how many stores we hit, we couldn't get our hands on that exact doll, and we knew nothing else would do for her. We called dozens of stores but couldn't find it anywhere. We checked online but people were selling the doll at ridiculous prices, as if it were some kind of collector's item and not a piece of cheap plastic in a fabric dress."

He chuckled softly. "Crazy, right? I remember desperately wanting a Tickle Me Elmo toy for Christmas when I was a kid. I didn't get it, although I sincerely doubt my mom put much effort into finding one." Marcus's voice lowered, rough with bitterness, and Sarah knew why.

His mother was an alcoholic who'd abandoned her family when Marcus was five. Unless something had changed in the years since Sarah had last seen him, he hadn't heard from his mother even once since she left, not even when he graduated from high school.

And as if that wasn't enough trauma for a child to go through, his dad had died in a tractor accident when he was nine, leaving him and his older brother, Matt, to be raised by Sheryl, his grandmother on his father's side of the family. She was a faithful and kind woman who'd given him a good Christian upbringing and had showered him with love. At the end of the day, his grandma had turned out to be a great blessing to him, but Sarah didn't blame him for harboring a bit of resentment in his heart toward his mother. He'd been through a lot.

"I remember Elmo, too. What a silly little toy that was. The doll Onyx wanted had a different cry for when she was wet or hungry."

"A doll that bawls when she gets hungry? That sounds kind of creepy to me."

Sarah nodded. She agreed wholeheartedly about that doll and she hated it for what it represented. Justin's death. Her deep and abiding sense of loneliness. Even though she still had a loving family surrounding her, sometimes she felt as if she were all alone in the universe. Even her prayers seemed to bounce back at her.

"On the morning of Christmas Eve, we got a call from a local toy shop in Golden. They had one doll available if we could get into town before the store closed. I told Justin that I didn't think it was worth going out in the storm. The weather conditions were terrible. Onyx had plenty of other gifts to open. She wouldn't have felt deprived. But he was always a stubborn man, and he insisted he could make it if he went out on his ATV. He would have done anything for his precious little girl."

Marcus nodded.

"He phoned me when he made it to town safely and picked up the doll for Onyx." She could barely force the words through her dry lips. "He said the roads weren't as bad as he'd thought they would be and not to worry about him. But he never made it back. He hit a patch of black ice on the road and slid into a tree. Died instantly."

Marcus reached for her again, and this time she let him envelop her free hand in his large, steady one. He pulled her gently to her feet, careful not to wake Jewel, who was now sleeping in the crook of her arm.

He swept a stray lock of hair behind her ear and let his palm linger on her cheek. "I'm so, so sorry for everything you've suffered. My heart goes out to you. And it explains a lot."

She wasn't sure what he meant. Explained what?

She tried to read his gaze, but it contained such a mixture of emotions that she couldn't even begin to sort them out and make any sense of them.

Truthfully, she was afraid to try.

She wondered if he could feel her tremble under his touch as he brushed the pad of his thumb across her cheekbone.

"I'm going to make you a promise right here and

now," he declared, his voice raspy. He put the palm of her hand on his chest, over his heart, which was beating rapidly. "I won't leave this house until you're certain it's safe for me to do so. Okay?"

His thoughtfulness overwhelmed her and she blinked back the tears stinging her eyes. "What about Christmas? Isn't your grandmother expecting you?"

His smile returned, gentle yet confident. "I'm sure she'll understand. Besides, I've still got a couple of days yet, and it's only a ten-hour drive to get to Grandma Sheryl's ranch. Twelve if I stop for meals and to stretch my legs. Plenty of time to make it home for the holidays."

He reached for his cell phone in his back pocket. "I should probably call her before it gets too late and let her know I'll be staying over here tonight. That way she won't worry and she'll know when to expect me."

He glanced at his cell and frowned. "Hmm. No bars." He held the phone above his head and did a little dance, walking around and waving his arm in an attempt to find better reception.

"The storm is probably messing with the cell tower. You may have to step out on the porch to get any bars. I sometimes find better reception when I go outside. Bundle up, though, or you'll freeze to death out there."

He winked at her. "No need. I'll only be a moment." He strode to the front door, yanked on his boots and put on his hat. He ducked his head as he stepped out into the blizzard, only looking back long enough to grin at her and make a shivering motion with his arms.

As he closed the door, she could hear him laughing. It had been a long time since there had been laughter in the house.

Far too long.

Chapter Three

There was no cell phone reception at Sarah's ranch. None. Zero. Zip.

Not inside the cabin and definitely not outside in the bitter cold. The freezing wind was blowing snow down the collar of his shirt and he was turning into an icicle. He should have listened to Sarah when she'd told him to bundle up. His thick wool coat would be a welcome commodity right now, but he'd intended to be outside for only a moment. The joke was on him.

He'd intended to dial Grandma Sheryl to touch base with her. Assure her he was safe and that he'd still be home for Christmas. Let her know that he was still planning to bring the horses as soon as the snow let up. While he was on the phone, he'd also wanted to ask her why she'd purchased Sarah's draft horses—and speaking of Sarah, why Grandma had failed to mention that the horses belonged to his high school sweetheart. That couldn't possibly have been an oversight on her part, and Marcus was more than a little bit suspicious that this whole setup was part of some misguided matchmaking scheme Grandma Sheryl had concocted.

If only she knew just how far off she was.

He waved his phone in the air one more time for good measure, praying for even a single bar to pop up. He wasn't surprised when he got nothing. At this rate it would be a blessing if he even managed to make it home in time for the holidays.

He especially didn't want to miss out on Christmas this year. According to Grandma Sheryl, his older brother, Matt, was already at the ranch. There had been tension between the two boys since the day their father died. They weren't close. The whole family hadn't been together in years. Though he doubted Matt felt the same way about him, Marcus was looking forward to seeing his brother again, even if things remained strained between them—and even if he had to share news from their mother that might serve to pull them further apart. Their mother had recently contacted Marcus and wanted to reconcile with him and Matt. It was certainly not the type of thing one said over the phone.

He envied Matt, who was already at the ranch with Grandma, enjoying her homemade cookies and fudge. His mouth was watering already. They were going to be worried if they didn't hear from him, but there wasn't a single thing he could do about it, short of sending smoke signals. Hopefully the storm would die down by tomorrow and he'd be able to be on his way.

Despite the deep longing to be home for Christmas, the thought of driving away from Sarah clouded his chest with emotion. It had been so many years since they'd seen each other. At one time she'd been the most important person in the world to him. Now that they'd run across each other's paths again, or more accurately, had been craftily thrown together by his mischievous grandmother, it seemed a shame just to leave without renewing their acquaintance. Much had happened to him during the years they'd been apart, and he imagined she had many stories to tell, as well.

Then again, maybe they would do little more than exchange numbers and stay in touch this time, and not let twelve years go by without seeing one another as they had last time. Could they even be friends now?

"Where's the baby?" he asked as he returned to the cabin, welcoming the warmth that enveloped his frosty limbs. He shivered and rubbed his hands over his biceps. He expected Sarah to come back with an "I told you so," but she didn't say a word.

She was still seated on the raggedy armchair, her elbows propped on her knees. Her somber gaze was fastened to the contents inside the coffee mug she held clasped in her hands, and the slight hint of a frown hovered on her lips. She appeared as if she were searching for answers in the depths of the black liquid.

She looked up, her eyes shaded by dark circles. "Asleep. I put her down in her crib for a nap."

"Wait—didn't she just wake up from a nap?"

She chuckled drily. "Babies have a fairly predictable rhythm. Sleep, eat, soil their diapers. Wash, rinse, repeat. Pretty much twenty-four hours a day at first, which is why parents of newborns usually look so ragged. It's better now that she's six months old—she is awake for longer periods and interacts with her surroundings. Still, I think all the excitement might have been too much for her."

Was that why Sarah appeared so world weary? Because she had to care for her baby twenty-four/seven?

"Parents have to be available according to the baby's cycle," she continued, "even in the middle of the night."

Her gray eyes lightened to the color of heather. Her gaze was tender, and just the smallest hint of a smile played about her lips.

Marcus took a breath. It was a relief to see her countenance brighten, even if it was only a shadow of the woman he'd once known.

"You'll experience all the sleep deprivation firsthand when you become a father."

His gut knotted. A father? He still held a grudge with his own mother a mile long and wasn't absolutely convinced he would succeed as a parent where his own had failed. Still, he remembered a time when he'd wondered what it would be like to be a dad—to Sarah's children. He might even have been able to overcome his apprehension, if their lives had taken a different turn.

After she'd broken up with him, he'd put all notions of a wife and family aside. He'd told himself that it wasn't because of Sarah, that his feelings must not have been any deeper than a teenage infatuation. Yet in all the years since, he hadn't had one single long-term relationship. He was a social person and he dated a lot, but conscientiously backed off at the first sign that a woman might be getting serious about him. He didn't want to hurt anyone's feelings. He just wasn't in it for the whole race. He was perfectly content in his career working with the teenage boys at Redemption Ranch down in Serendipity, Texas—or at least he'd thought he had been.

Until today.

Now he couldn't help but wonder—what might life have been like for him and Sarah, if things had turned out differently? If she hadn't broken his heart?

He'd always known Sarah would be a wonderful mom. She was sweet and kind right down to her bones.

The fact that she put Jewel's needs before her own without a second thought didn't surprise him at all, nor did it astonish him when she spoke of getting up in the middle of the night to care for her child as if it was a privilege and not a chore. Despite the stress she was obviously feeling at celebrating the holiday without her spouse, her expression softened whenever she spoke of her children.

She glanced up and met his gaze, a smile still lingering on her lips. "Were you able to get a hold of Sheryl?"

He shook his head and sat on the couch facing her, leaning forward and clasping his hands on his lap. "Nope. No service. I couldn't get a single bar."

"That happens a lot up here, especially when there's a storm. I hope your grandma doesn't worry about you."

"Me, too. Although in this case I suspect she might not be surprised that I'm lingering, with or without the weather acting up. But I hate putting an extra burden on her."

"An *extra* burden?" she repeated. She studied his face as if looking for an answer in his expression.

He'd said too much already. He pressed his lips and raised his brow. There was no need to get into his issues when she had enough of her own to deal with.

"You can tell me to mind my own business if you want, but I have the distinct impression you aren't just talking about the delay caused by the snowstorm, are you?"

Well, one thing hadn't changed from the time they'd been dating. She could still read him like a book.

"I wish I could say the storm was all that was worrying me, but that's not entirely accurate." He reached for the mug sitting on the end table beside him and took a sip of coffee Sarah had rewarmed for him, telling himself the burning in his throat was the result of the hot liquid and not the emotions roiling through him.

"Is Sheryl ill?" Her voice raised in alarm.

"No, nothing like that. I didn't mean to worry you. Grandma's in perfect health, thank the Lord. It's my mother."

"Oh." Sarah inhaled with an audible gasp. "What happened to her?"

"Nothing happened to her," he corrected, shaking his head. "It's more what happened to me. She called me a couple of weeks ago, right out of the blue. After all these years, she just phoned me and expected me to speak with her."

"What did she want?"

"Reconciliation, I think. To be part of my life and Matt's again, as if she can just waltz back in and take her place in our family like she never left. It was like a punch in the gut. Still is. I guess she decided to reach out to me and not Matt because I'm the sucker of the bunch."

"No, you are not," she exclaimed, rising to her feet and planting her hands on her hips. "Marcus Ender, I don't ever want to hear you speak that way about yourself again. You are the nicest man I've ever met. If your mother chose to call you, it's because she knows how kindhearted you are. That is *not* a bad trait to have. You should be proud of yourself."

"She doesn't know *anything* about me," he retorted bitterly, staring down at his clenched fists, squeezing them until it hurt. "She was long gone before she had the chance to find out what kind of man I'd become."

"No, you're right. I spoke in haste." Sarah dropped onto the couch next to him and tucked one leg underneath her so she was facing him. "She doesn't deserve a son like you."

Despite the fact that speaking about his mother always renewed the feeling that his heart had been chewed up and spit out, he was vibrantly aware of Sarah's nearness, of her arm around his shoulders and the gentleness and understanding in her eyes. The air between them snapped with electricity.

She got him, right to the depths of his being. She was the only one who ever had. The realization was accompanied by an inexplicable feeling of loss.

"I can see where you think she might be taking advantage of you." Sarah's voice rippled along the pathway of his nerves.

"You don't think she is?"

He didn't know why he was sharing such intimate details of his life with her, except that he needed to unburden himself and she'd been a solid rock for him during his turbulent teenage years. Until today he hadn't told a single soul about his conversation with his mother, not even his best friend, Tessa, who worked as the girls' counselor at Redemption Ranch. He was proud of the work he'd done at Redemption Ranch, but being the counselor—the one who helped others through their problems—sometimes made him feel as if he wasn't allowed to have problems of his own. Everyone expected him to have the answers and to be the strong one. And at times—times such as now—he just didn't know how.

Somehow it felt right to unload his anxieties to Sarah. He'd depended on her in high school and he trusted her now. How well he remembered graduation day. Sarah had stood by him as he'd waited in vain for his mother to appear, hoped beyond hope that that would be the day she would change and realize the importance of family. Sarah had held his hand while he'd wept wounded tears.

"She says she's sober." He scoffed and shook his head. "She wants to meet up with me first and then eventually with Matt. Maybe try to repair some of what's been broken."

"How do you feel about that?"

He grunted. "I don't know. Most of the time I'm too angry to even consider the possibility, but sometimes I can't help but wonder. No matter what she's done, she's still my mother."

Sarah absently brushed her hand across his shoulder. "She's put you between a rock and a hard place, that's for sure."

"Right? And somehow I have to figure out what's best for the whole family. I have to find a way to let Matt and Grandma Sheryl know that she wants to be a part of our lives. Matt's going to be furious. I just hope he doesn't take it out on me."

"Can you find it in your heart to forgive her, do you think? Allow her to be a part of your life, even if your brother wants nothing to do with her?"

He blew out a breath and winced. That was the question he'd been asking himself for a week, and he wasn't any closer to an answer now than he had been back then. "I don't know, Sarah. I honestly don't know."

Sarah's heart went out to Marcus. His mother had really done a number on him. She'd let her family down in the worst possible way, abandoning them and walking away without looking back. She was an alcoholic, which explained her actions but didn't absolve them.

She could see the pain in Marcus's eyes and felt it as if it were her own. His mother's sudden return to his life was ripping his heart out. She wasn't the least bit surprised that the woman had approached Marcus and not his bad-boy brother, Matt. Marcus was tender-hearted. He always tried to do the right thing—but what the *right thing* was in this situation was difficult to call.

Sarah's first impulse was to suggest he toss his mom out on her ear should she dare to show up in person. She didn't deserve any better than that, and it would spare Marcus from any additional pain she might cause. But that wasn't Marcus's way.

"What are you going to do?" she asked, sweeping her hand over the tense muscles of his shoulders and coming to land on his arm. His biceps tightened. Time had certainly worked in his favor in that regard. She didn't remember him being so strong when she'd dated him in high school.

"Honestly? I don't know. I told her I'd try to broach the subject with Grandma Sheryl and Matt, but I already know they won't be too keen to hear the news that mom is suddenly *ready* for us. I highly doubt reconciliation will be on the menu, at least not for a long time to come."

"Are you planning to meet up with her?"

"No." He shook his head fervently and then shrugged. "I don't know. Maybe. Better I step forward than deny her and have her end up going after Matt. If I see her face-to-face, I'll know right away if she's lying about turning her life around. I suppose that'll give me a better idea about what I should do next."

Sarah opened her mouth to offer her support and then clamped it shut again. Surely he had many people in his life who would stand up with him during this trial—if not his family, then at least some close friends. He was nothing if not a social being. She was in a bad place in her life right now. She had nothing to offer him. And as for the two of them—

Well, there was no *two of them*. Not anymore.

She was still debating on what she should say to him when the lights flickered. She groaned.

His gaze widened. "Are we going to—"

He never finished his sentence. The lights flared once, she heard a loud bang and then everything went dark. It was twilight outside and there was still a small measure of gray light pouring in from the windows, but she knew it would be only a matter of minutes before they would be cast into the pitch-blackness of mountain living.

"Electrical outage?" Marcus asked.

She nodded. Onyx darted into the room, clutching her stuffed brown bunny and whimpering. "I heard a scary sound, Mama."

Before Sarah could say a word, Marcus crossed the room and held out his hands to the little girl. Onyx didn't hesitate. She climbed right into his arms and clung to his neck.

"It's okay, little darlin'," Marcus assured the three-year-old. One side of his mouth crept upward as he met Sarah's gaze. That crooked grin had always made her heartbeat quicken, and now was no exception. She'd never found him more attractive in her life than in the moment he stepped in to console her child. "We're going to play a little game right now. It'll be fun. Do you like flashlights?"

Onyx nodded and Marcus shifted her to one side so he could dig into the front pocket of his jeans. He withdrew his key chain and pressed the button on a tiny silver flashlight, waving the beam toward the wall so Onyx could see the light dance against the shadows.

"Can you be a big girl and hold the flashlight for your mama and me while we gather some supplies together? It'll be just like camping out. Do you like to camp?"

Onyx squealed in delight as Marcus handed her the flashlight and showed her how to use it. For not the first time that day, Sarah's eyes burned with unshed tears. During the summertime, Justin had often taken the family fishing and hiking. They were some of Sarah's fondest memories, although she doubted Onyx was old enough to recall such outings.

"Do you have a backup generator?" he asked, directing the question to Sarah. "How long do you think it will be before the electrical company can get the power back up?"

"We had a generator when the farm was doing well. After Justin passed away, I had to sell it."

He studied her, his golden eyebrows lowering.

She tipped her chin and squared her shoulders. She knew he'd picked up on what she'd said—or rather, hadn't said—about the debts she owed, but she refused to let him pity her.

"I'm not sure about the power company," she continued. "It might take a while. It sounded like something major blew up just before the lights went out. A transformer, maybe? Once a couple of years ago I remember when a drunk driver rammed his truck into a transformer near the farm. We were without power for a week. I had to do all my cooking in the fireplace.

"We ate a lot of hot dogs that week." She chuckled. "But that was in the middle of the summer, so it wasn't quite so bad, temperature-wise. A little stuffy in the daytime, but it still got chilly at night. But now we're stranded in a snowstorm."

He nodded in agreement. "It's going to get cold in here."

Freezing cold, like an icebox. And fast. She focused on her breathing, refusing to give in to the panic rising in her chest. "I guess the first order of business is going to be lighting a fire in the hearth. Marcus, if you wouldn't mind gathering an armful of logs, I'll pull together some old newspapers for kindling. There should be some wood stacked in the bin just outside the back door. Through the kitchen and then to the right." She pointed to the kitchen and crooked her finger to indicate which way he should go.

"I'll wear my coat this time," he said, winking at Sarah as he plopped Onyx onto the armchair. "Will you keep holding that light for your mama while I'm gone?" he asked the child, who beamed up at him as if he held the sun in the sky. "You're a big girl. Your mama really depends on your help."

Sarah shivered at the icy breeze that blew through the house when Marcus opened the back door and stepped outside. It was already several degrees cooler in the cabin, and the temperature was dropping at an alarming rate. She hoped Marcus would hurry in with the wood. She was already feeling a chill, and she had an infant and elderly parents-in-law to worry about. They'd be especially susceptible to the cold.

"Onyx, honey, let's go find Jewel, Pops and Granny. I'll bet they'll want to see the big, roaring fire Mr. Marcus is going to help us build."

"Can we cook hot dogs?" Onyx asked as they walked down the hall to where Jewel was napping. "And roast marshmallows?"

Sarah laughed. She hadn't seen Onyx's eyes light up like this in a very long time.

Too long.

"I think that's a great idea. I might even have some graham crackers and chocolate bars around here somewhere. We can make big, smushy s'mores for dessert."

"Yay! S'mores!"

Maybe Onyx remembered more about camping with her father than Sarah had imagined. That concerned her. She was ashamed to realize she hadn't put much effort into doing "fun" things with Onyx since Justin's death. She'd been so preoccupied with the debts and obligations her husband had left her that she hadn't spent the time she should have finding ways to make her daughter smile again.

She crouched down to give Onyx a hearty hug and kiss, but the girl quickly wriggled out of her grasp. Chuckling, Sarah stood and scooped Jewel from her crib, wrapping her in a warm blanket. Then she stopped by Pops and Granny's room to let them know about her plan to light a fire and congregate in the living room. She also suggested they both throw on an extra layer of clothing. Pops especially was vulnerable to the cold these days. His circulation wasn't what it used to be.

"We'll gather some blankets and be right with you," Granny assured her. Pops simply grunted his assent.

Sarah returned to the living room, expecting Marcus to be hunched over the hearth lighting the fire, but there was no sign of him. Where was he with the firewood? Surely it couldn't take him that long to grab an armful of logs from just outside the back door.

She entered the kitchen with Jewel propped on her hip and Onyx following close behind her, waving the beam of light across the walls and exclaiming in delight at the shadows it made. Sarah pulled the curtain aside to peek out into the backyard.

To her surprise, Marcus wasn't on the porch. He'd shed his coat and was angling an ax at a slab of wood he'd perched on the chopping block.

Why was he chopping logs? Didn't they have any wood in the bin? To her dismay, she suddenly remembered she'd used the last of it in October during the first big snowstorm of the year. She'd been meaning to refill the bin, but time had gotten away from her and she'd forgotten all about it.

And now poor Marcus was out there battling the elements on her behalf. She was ashamed of herself for the oversight, but how much worse would it have been if Marcus *hadn't* been here? She would have been the one splitting logs in the whiteout, and she wasn't nearly as competent with an ax as Marcus appeared to be. She imagined his fingers and toes were turning icy with the cold, but he swung away regardless.

She breathed a prayer of thanksgiving for the Lord's provision, that He'd somehow orchestrated events so Marcus was here during the blackout. But poor Marcus!

She couldn't even make him a cup of hot cocoa to warm him up when he came inside. At least not until they had the fire going.

While she waited for Marcus, she tended to other things that needed doing, creating a mental checklist and ticking items off as she went. First up was digging out some old newspapers from the office for kindling. Then they needed blankets, flashlights and maybe even a few candles. She also had a couple of LED lanterns she kept in the hall closet for situations like this.

If the electricity remained out, and her gut instinct told her it would be a while before it came back on, they'd all need to sleep in the living room near the warmth of the fire. The couch folded out for the grandparents and she could blow up an air mattress for her and Onyx. Jewel would sleep in the porta-crib. But she had no idea what she was going to do with Marcus.

Speaking of Marcus…

She returned to the kitchen and glanced out the window to see how he was doing. He was still chopping away. Despite the weather, he'd shed his coat and sweat glistened on his brow. She couldn't help but admire the way his muscles contracted and released with every swing of the ax. His jaw was set tight and he was striking the wood with fervency that Sarah sensed went beyond just the desire to be back inside where it was warm.

No—it was more than that. Maybe he was releasing his stress from their conversation about his mother. Or was it being here with her that was causing him concern? They hadn't anticipated encountering each other after all these years, and he hadn't planned to stay cloistered in the cabin with her and her family until the weather had given him no other choice in the matter.

Now not only were they stranded, but he'd have no option but to be thrown together with her entire brood in order to stay warm. Nothing like being a confirmed bachelor locked in with an ex-girlfriend, a cranky old couple, a fussy baby and a raucous preschooler. Marcus was a nice guy—the best—but this situation went beyond inconvenient and straight into uncomfortable.

She returned to the living room and set up the porta-crib so Jewel could amuse herself with her toys. Onyx was still playing with the flashlight, and Sarah could hear Carl and Eliza quietly spatting about something or other as they rummaged through the hall closet.

A couple of minutes later, Marcus shuffled in, his

arms loaded with wood for the fire. Tiny icicles glistened in his golden hair like a crown.

"I think the temperature dropped a good ten degrees just in the time I was out there," he said, dropping to his knees in front of the fireplace and carefully arranging the logs around wads of newspaper. "I filled up the bin just in case the blackout lasts beyond tonight."

"Thank you. And I'm so sorry," Sarah apologized.

"For what?"

"I didn't mean for you to have to chop all that wood yourself. When I sent you out, I'd forgotten that I used the last of what I had back in October during the first flurry. It just slipped my mind that I needed to chop some more logs and refill the bin."

He leaned back in a catcher's crouch, bracing his forearms on his knees as he watched the fire roar to life. He glanced back, grinning at Sarah.

"Trust me, it was no problem. My long legs have been cramped in my truck for two days. I enjoyed getting the chance to stretch and swing the ax. That little bit of exercise did me good."

"Well, I apologize just the same. Now, why don't you relax by the fire for a while?"

He stood so fast that she didn't even see him coming. He took her by the shoulders and guided her to the easy chair, gently pressing her into it. He spoke sweet nonsense words to Jewel as he picked her up and placed her on Sarah's lap. "You're the one who needs to relax."

"But I've got to scrounge something up for dinner. Open a few cans of whatever I've got in the pantry."

"Nope," he said, holding his hands palm out to stem her flow of words. "I don't think so."

Chapter Four

Marcus wasn't about to sit around and let Sarah do all the work while he lounged by the fire.

"You sit tight and take care of those beautiful children of yours. I'll get supper on for us."

"You don't have to do that."

He flashed her a toothy grin. "I know. I want to."

"Oh. Well, then…" She didn't appear to have the energy to argue with him, which was just exactly why he wanted to take care of her right now. Er—take care of the *meal*. Sarah had enough on her proverbial plate just watching out after her family.

"Hot dogs. I want a hot dog," Onyx exclaimed, jumping up and down and clapping her hands.

He laughed and gave the child a friendly bow. "Hot dogs it is, little lady. Your wish is my command."

He paused and raised an eye at Sarah. "Guess I should have asked first—do we have hot dogs?"

"In the meat drawer. Try not to keep the refrigerator door open too long or you'll let out all the cold air."

He winked. "We wouldn't want cold air in the house, now, would we?"

She chuckled. "You know what I mean."

"Yeah, darlin', I do."

"I also have marshmallows, graham crackers and chocolate bars in the pantry."

"S'mores." He smacked his lips exaggeratedly. "Sounds like a meal to me."

"Sounds like *dessert*," Sarah corrected, wagging a finger at him. "After a healthy, well-balanced meal."

He burst into a hearty laugh. Marcus had the most contagious laughter of anyone she'd ever known, and it wasn't long before everyone in the room joined in.

"We may have to resort to canned fruits and vegetables to round out the meal," Sarah said. "We had fresh apples and green grapes in a basket on the kitchen table, but I think they may be gone by now. The grapes, anyway. Little fingers love to sneak a few when Mama's not looking."

Eliza murmured something to Sarah and Marcus headed to the kitchen. It didn't take him long to scrounge up a meal, with no cans included or necessary. A quick glance into the refrigerator brought him cheese, bread and the package of hot dogs Onyx had requested. It made him happy to make that little girl smile.

There were a few apples left in the basket on the table. Not enough for everyone to have one, but he could cut them into slices with a paring knife.

Rummaging through the pantry for the goodies for the s'mores, he stumbled across a picnic basket. He looked inside and discovered a red-checked tablecloth and plastic plates, cups and utensils. Perfect. An idea of how to make the adventure more fun for everyone popped fully formed into his mind.

Grinning, he packed his stash in the basket, including a bottle of sparkling cider and a couple of large wooden skewers that would be just right for cooking hot dogs over an open flame.

"Anyone up for a picnic?" he called as he entered the living room. "I've got hot dogs. And fixings for s'mores."

"I am, I am," Onyx exclaimed. It seemed to Marcus that once the child started talking, she had two volumes—loud and louder. He liked everything about her. She was the cutest little thing he'd ever seen. Well, maybe after her mother.

He glanced at Sarah, who mouthed a silent, "Thank you." He grinned and nodded. It was his pleasure. Truly.

While Marcus assisted Onyx in cooking her hot dog over the fire, Sarah laid out all the goodies on the red-checked tablecloth, which she spread across the floor in front of the coffee table. She even lit a couple of fragrant green pillar candles that filled the room with the pleasant scent of pine trees. Fitting, considering where they were.

Carl offered a blessing, and conversation hummed as they shared their simple meal together. Carl and Eliza were full of stories about the Christmas tree farm. They spoke of their love for the guests who visited with such nostalgia it put an ache in Marcus's heart. Clearly they weren't running the business this year. Justin's death had hit them all hard. They were good people. He wished there was some way he could bring some joy back into their lives.

Sarah regaled him with some crazy antics involving the reindeer, Snort and Crash. Onyx loved the horses and riding in the sleigh.

Marcus swallowed around the lump in his throat

when he realized he was here to take the horses away. What kind of Christmas present was that?

No. He couldn't do that to the little girl, or to her mama. He wouldn't. He'd call up Grandma Sheryl as soon as his cell phone service turned back on and tell her he was leaving the Percherons right where they were. He'd pay her back with his own money and purchase another team of draft horses for Grandma, if it came to that.

Just not *this* team. Mag and Jes belonged here, pulling the Kendrickses' sleigh.

It was only two days until Christmas. Tomorrow was Christmas Eve. If he left first thing in the morning he'd barely make it home by Christmas Day—and that was a big *if* since the snow didn't show signs of stopping. For all he knew he'd be stranded here all the way through the holiday. And like the little drummer boy, he had no gift to bring—but he could give Sarah and all of the Kendrickses part of their holiday back. Maybe they could all go on a sleigh ride once the weather let up a bit. Rev things up and get some Christmas cheer going. Cookies. Eggnog. Carols.

Come to think of it, Marcus realized there was something missing from the Kendrickses' house.

Christmas.

Not a tree. Not a wreath. Not a single decoration. How odd that the farm was entirely dedicated to the holiday and the cabin was so decidedly *not* in the Christmas spirit.

He understood why, of course, and the reason tugged at his heart. They were all still grieving for Justin. Christmas, especially, would remind them of his passing. But that wasn't a good reason to sweep the whole season under the rug.

Christmas wasn't just about Santa Claus and boughs of holly and presents under the tree. It was about remembering Christ's humble birth and that someday He would return again.

As a teenager Sarah had been a woman of amazing faith. She'd opened Marcus's eyes and heart to a deeper relationship with God, one that he carried with him to this day.

As he set out a board game for Onyx, he cast a furtive glance in her direction, studying her as she picked up the plates. Sarah's faith had obviously been tested to the edge of her breaking point with all that had happened to her. Did she still cling to her faith in God to get her through the worst of her trials?

It wasn't as if he could ask her such a personal question, especially not with her family around her, so instead he turned his attention to Onyx and the game they were playing. The object was to remove bones and organs from a cartoon man using only a set of tweezers. If either of them hit the metal on the side, the fellow's big red nose would light up and buzz loudly.

Marcus had a steady hand and knew he could easily remove the pieces, but he wasn't certain Onyx had developed her fine motor skills enough to handle the tweezers properly.

It took him about thirty seconds to realize his concern didn't matter. For a three-year-old, the joy came in *making* the man's nose light up. The more it buzzed, the harder Onyx giggled.

When it was Marcus's turn—using a very loose definition of *turn*—he made the fellow buzz and wiggled around as if he'd been zapped by a bolt of electricity, causing everyone in the room to chuckle at his antics.

In some ways he felt as if he *had* been zapped by a bolt of electricity—the moment he'd met Sarah on the road.

He ruffled Onyx's hair as Eliza spread out a new board game for the little girl.

"I'm going to see how your mama is faring in the kitchen," he told her. "I'm sure she can use some help washing all those dishes."

Eliza eyed him over her rectangular reading glasses, reminding him once again of Mrs. Claus. Clearly she didn't buy his excuse. A handful of plastic plates, cups and utensils hardly qualified as a load of dishes.

He spent an uncomfortable moment waiting for Eliza's assent, meeting her pale blue eyes square-on and opening his heart to her gaze.

After what seemed like forever but was probably only a few seconds, she clicked her tongue and waved him away. "What are you waiting for, then, son? She'll be needing your assistance, for sure." Her voice held a trace of sarcasm and yet was couched in goodwill. Marcus suspected that was just her way of dealing with the world, and he flashed his most charming smile at her before he left the room.

She snorted and shook her head but her cheeks were stained a pretty pink color. His grin widened and he mentally patted himself on the back. Oh, yeah. He still had it with the ladies.

Except for Sarah.

She had her back turned to him as he entered the kitchen, her arms elbow-deep in a sudsy sink full of water.

"Can I help?" he asked at the same moment he set his hands on her shoulders.

She shrieked and whirled on him, tossing the baby food bowl she'd been washing, which was filled to the brim with water. He was instantly soaked, all down the front of his shirt.

"Don't *do* that," she said, laying a wet palm over her heart.

"I'm sorry," he said at the same time. They both laughed.

"Sorry I soaked you," she said, picking up a dish towel and dabbing at his shirt. "But you really shouldn't sneak up on people that way. You nearly scared the life out of me. My heart is racing a million miles a second."

He smirked and waggled his eyebrows. "I've been told I have that effect on women."

"Oh, you." She popped him with the dish towel.

In turn, he scooped up a handful of bubbles from the sink and crowned her head with them. She squealed and tried to wriggle away from him but he was too fast for her. With little effort on his part, he snatched the dish towel away from her.

She reached for it but he held it over his head, out of her reach, and danced away with a chuckle. Then he draped the towel over his shoulder and mock bowed to her. "You wash. I'll dry."

"You say the most romantic things."

He knew she meant it to be a teasing remark, but the moment their eyes met Marcus felt as if someone had pulled all the oxygen from the room. His lungs weren't functioning and he was fairly certain his heart wasn't beating.

She was so beautiful. He could get lost in her glimmering gray eyes, which reflected the glow of the candles she'd lit in order to make her way around the kitchen. Her expression sweetened as the flickering candlelight erased the lines of strain around her eyes and mouth.

He framed her face with his palms and brushed his thumbs across the silky skin covering her cheekbones. She gasped softly and her gaze drifted to his lips. She covered his hands with hers.

He could almost hear the soundtrack, the swell of the silent symphony that matched the expanse of emotion in his chest.

"Sarah, I—"

She didn't let him finish. Her eyes widened to epic proportions and she clamped a hand over her mouth, physically rejecting the movement they both knew would soon follow.

Smart girl. Smarter than him, anyway, to think he could just step back in time twelve years and pick up where they'd left off. He knew better than that. Apparently, so did she.

"Sarah, I—" he began again, feeling as if he should apologize, even though technically nothing had happened.

Nothing except that he'd almost given her his heart again, forgetting that she'd never wanted it in the first place.

She grabbed the towel off his shoulder and shoved it at his chest. "You've got some catching up to do, cowboy."

So that was it, then. Pretend it didn't happen. Marcus knew he couldn't do that, but for now he followed her lead, picking up one of the plastic plates she'd washed and patting it dry with the towel.

"I heard a lot of buzzing going on out there," she said, her tone awkwardly conversational. "And a lot of laughter. I take it you're not very good at that game."

"I'll have you know that I *rock* that game. But Onyx showed me it was much more fun to make the dude's nose light up."

"You're good with her."

Marcus thought her statement would be punctuated with a smile, but instead her full lips bowed downward.

"What?" he asked, confused. "Is that a bad thing? I really enjoy spending time with your family. I never had that growing up."

"I know," she said, her voice unusually low and thick. She eyed him and gnawed on her bottom lip, a habit Marcus remembered as a sign that she was nervous. But what did she have to be nervous about?

"I'm glad you're enjoying your time with my family, and your presence here today has been a real blessing to all of us."

Well, he was glad to hear that. For a moment there he thought she might be ready to toss him out on his ear, snow or no snow.

"But?" he questioned, because there was definitely a qualifier on its way.

"Just—just don't get too attached," she stammered. "Okay?"

Sarah's stomach churned as Marcus's expressive eyes went from confused to wounded. She didn't mean to hurt his feelings, but there was more at stake than just the emotional roller coast Marcus had put her on.

She had her children to consider, Onyx in particular. For some reason the little girl had really taken to Marcus. Sarah supposed she wasn't surprised that he'd charmed his way into Onyx's heart, but it was still amazing to watch the way he gently coaxed her out of the shell she'd built around herself, something Sarah hadn't been able to do.

Part of it, she supposed, was that, as he'd explained over dinner, he was trained as a counselor. That didn't surprise her. He'd always been empathetic. But mostly it was just Marcus being Marcus—sweet, honest, open Marcus.

Even now, as she pressed freshly roasted, perfectly browned marshmallows on top of squares of chocolate and sandwiched them in between graham crackers, Marcus was entertaining Onyx by making bunny shadows on the wall.

"Bunnies are my favorite animal," Onyx declared, punctuating her sentence with a squeal.

"Yeah, I got that." Sarah could *hear* him smiling even though she was on the other side of the room.

"Buttons is my real bunny." She thrust her stuffed rabbit under Marcus's nose. "This is Brownie. Mama lets me sleep with Brownie."

Marcus chuckled. "Like the dessert?"

"Like the color," Sarah inserted, offering him the plate of s'mores. "She also has Whitey the horse and Pinky the elephant. It's a thing when you're three."

"Unique," he said, smiling down at Onyx. "I never would have thought of that."

Onyx beamed. She was eating up his attention—and that was the problem. It wasn't so much that she minded Marcus showering her daughter with genuine affection. She'd never been great at that and she could tell how much Onyx missed her daddy, but she didn't want her little girl getting confused.

Anyone with eyes could see Onyx was getting attached to Marcus. She clearly adored him and he seemed to feel the same way about her. He'd even taken the time to rescue Buttons the Bunny, bringing him, hutch and all, into the living room for some much-needed warmth. But he'd be leaving after the snow abated and who knew when, if ever, they would see each other again.

She refused to analyze the emotions that rose up to clog her throat. It was concern for Onyx, nothing more.

If only that were true. She'd never felt so mixed up in her life. There in the kitchen, that moment when he'd almost kissed her—she'd *wanted* him to kiss her. There was no doubt in her mind that she would have kissed him back. It had been a long time since she'd been held. Cherished. In Marcus's arms she felt the weight of the world lift off her shoulders.

She remembered how sweet his kisses were back when he was eighteen. She couldn't imagine how much they might have improved now that he'd matured into a man.

That scared the socks off her. What if Carl or Eliza had walked in on them—or worse yet, Onyx? She would never have been able to explain what had been going on at that moment because she didn't know herself.

As everyone enjoyed their s'mores, Sarah silently rocked Jewel to sleep, enjoying her infant scent and baby gurgles. The one thing she knew for certain was that Marcus's presence had changed her perspective on her family, reminding her that even though she'd lost Justin, she still had her two beautiful daughters to shower her love on. She'd needed that encouragement, and she was grateful both to God and to Marcus for providing it.

Sarah tucked the now-sleeping Jewel into her porta-crib. Marcus pulled out the hideaway bed from the couch and outfitted it with sheets and blankets, then took Eliza's arm as she tiredly shuffled her way over to the bed. Her arthritis was acting up again and Marcus seemed to sense her need for extra assistance, which he gave without a word. Eliza would have bristled if he'd made a big deal of it, but his gentleness won her over.

Carl tucked himself into the other side of the hideaway and groaned about the lack of padding.

"Hopefully it'll just be for one night, Pops," Sarah said, consoling him. "Better a little bit uncomfortable than freezing to death, right?"

"Mmm," Carl muttered. She couldn't tell whether he was agreeing with or disputing her statement but she never had the chance to ask, because he'd already drifted off to sleep, with Eliza close behind.

Marcus's smile was a tiny bit crooked, the only minor imperfection in his features. Sarah loved that smile.

He crouched and banked the fire. "Three down, one to go. Where do you plan on putting Onyx?"

"I pulled out our air mattress but I haven't pumped it up yet. I figured Onyx and I could share it, but I'm not sure..."

"...what to do with me." He gave the logs one last poke with the fire iron and then stood and gestured toward the easy chair. "Don't give it a second's thought. I'll just park myself right there in that chair."

Sarah chewed on her lip. "It won't be very comfortable, I'm afraid."

"Nonsense. I'll sleep like a baby. Better even than Jewel, I'll warrant. Don't forget I was raised on a ranch. I've spent many a night out under the stars with nothing more beneath me than a sleeping bag. Compared to that, this chair is comfy cozy."

The old, beat-up piece of furniture was the furthest thing from cozy, but she didn't know what else to do with him. At least he'd be near the fire.

In no time, she and Marcus had the air mattress filled and outfitted with a down comforter. They worked well together, not speaking, but not carrying on in an uncomfortable silence, either.

He'd helped her out a lot today. She was glad he was here, and if she was being honest with herself, she wasn't looking forward to tomorrow, to his imminent departure.

Onyx wasn't the only one becoming attached to Marcus. He'd changed the whole tenor of the house. Brought joy in his wake. Even Carl and Eliza were responding to his kindness, and that said a lot.

"You ready for bed, little lady?" Marcus asked Onyx. "I imagine it's already well past your normal bedtime."

"But I want to stay up with you and Mama," she whined, her bottom lip protruding. She looked adorable, and when she made that face Sarah always found it difficult not to give in to her wishes. From the heart-rending empathy in Marcus's expression, Sarah guessed that Onyx's pout was working on him.

Ha. Served him right. There was no guessing how many women over the years Marcus beguiled with his natural good looks and charm. Herself included—maybe her most of all. It only seemed fair that it was her own daughter who stole Marcus's heart away from him.

He cleared his throat and ran a hand back over his hair, sending golden curls sprouting out in every direction. "We're all going to go to sleep now, darlin'. I promise you won't miss a thing."

"Do you want to say your bedtime prayer now?" Sarah prompted.

Onyx nodded, and carefully setting aside her stuffed bunny, she took Sarah's hand—and then Marcus's. Sarah waited for the girl to begin. Usually she recited a fairly rote prayer of the preschool variety. But Onyx wasn't speaking. She was staring at Sarah's free hand.

Marcus figured it out before she did. He silently reached for her hand, interlocking their fingers and closing the prayer circle.

Onyx grinned and closed her eyes. "Dear Lord Jesus," she began, sounding as if she were composing a letter. "Thank You for today. Thank You for Pops and Granny and Mama and Jewel and Buttons." She paused before tacking on an addendum. "And thank You for Mr. Marcus."

His grip on Sarah's hand tightened. She glanced at him through hooded eyelids. His lips were pursed and his eyes squeezed tight. Was that a hint of moisture in the corner of his eye?

She felt as if she was trespassing on his private emotions and quickly closed her eyes again, waiting for Onyx to finish her prayer.

"Please watch over us and bless us. Sincerely, Onyx. Amen."

Sarah struggled not to chuckle at her daughter's eloquence.

"And thank You, Lord, for letting me share this time

with this wonderful family. Amen," Marcus added in a coarse whisper.

"Amen," Sarah repeated, feeling as if she should have somehow added to the prayer also but not knowing what to say. Onyx and Marcus had said it all.

Marcus squeezed her hand once more before untangling his fingers from hers. He made himself comfortable on the armchair while Sarah tucked Onyx in.

"Do you need an extra blanket?" she asked him. "A pillow, maybe?"

"Nope. I'm fine." He yawned for good measure, but Sarah thought he might be faking it.

She left the living room to grab Onyx's blankie from her bedroom and by the time she returned, Onyx had snuck out of bed and curled up in Marcus's lap, her arms clutching one of his and her head resting on his shoulder. It was a sight too precious for words, and for a moment Sarah forgot to breathe.

"Do you want me to move her?" Sarah whispered.

"No, not yet. Let's wait until she's fast asleep."

Sarah's throat clouded with emotion as she laid Onyx's blanket over both the man and the girl.

He pressed a kiss onto the top of Onyx's head and smiled softly as he met Sarah's gaze. His blue eyes were gleaming in the firelight.

"She's special," he murmured.

Sarah nodded. Words formed in her heart but she somehow managed to keep them from emerging from her lips and embarrassing the both of them.

So are you.

Chapter Five

Marcus did not sleep like a baby. In fact, he barely slept at all.

He'd kept Onyx on his lap far longer than was technically necessary. He'd never had a child respond to him quite as Onyx did, and it grabbed at his heart to think that she'd given him the privilege of putting her to sleep. He hadn't wanted to let her go, even though serving as her temporary mattress meant keeping too still for him to be able to nod off himself.

Even when he'd tucked the girl in next to her dozing mother, he hadn't been able to turn off his thoughts. He stared at the fire, ruminating over his day.

So this was what a family felt like. They weren't perfect. Everyone had their moments, their faults, and yet he sensed an overarching theme among them—love and acceptance. All of them, from the elderly Eliza to baby Jewel.

His own mother had deprived him and Matt of that kind of love. How could he ever forgive her for that, much less welcome her back into the family? Yet he wasn't going to be able to move on with his life until he'd made a decision on the matter. He only prayed he'd make the right one.

He'd never known the love of a family. Never thought he wanted to. Didn't think he cared whether or not he was raised by his parents or had to fend for himself. Grandma Sheryl had done her best, but she'd had the ranch to run, not leaving her much time to chase after Matt and Marcus, who were always running in different directions. He loved her and knew she loved him, but he didn't feel the need to connect with her on any deeper level. Didn't think it mattered that he and Matt weren't close and hadn't been since their father's death. But until today, he hadn't known what he was missing.

He must have dozed off at some point because he awoke to find the fire had gone out sometime during the night. It was still snowing, although not quite as hard as yesterday, and the cabin felt chilled. He wadded up more newspaper, fetched some logs and relit the fire, hoping to kick up the heat before anyone else woke up.

He slipped into his sheep's wool coat, put on his boots and hat and stepped outside to check for cell phone reception. His boots weren't ideal for the snow and he was slip-sliding all over the place, but instead of being a trial, it made him laugh. He could just picture Sarah coming out to look for him only to find he'd taken a nosedive into a snowbank.

He didn't have any bars on his phone so he walked around the exterior of the cabin to see if he could catch a signal. Still nothing.

He started to head back indoors, but then his eyes spotted the ax he'd lodged into the chopping block and a new idea hit him, charging his adrenaline and filling him with eager anticipation.

He could bring Christmas to the family. This was a Christmas tree farm, after all. What better place to find the perfect Christmas tree?

He stopped at the barn to feed the Percherons and the grunting reindeer. They sounded like a couple of pigs. Literally. And their legs clicked when they walked.

Click. Click. Click.

Weird. Who knew?

He didn't have far to hike to find some nice choices in evergreens. If anything, there were too many varieties to choose from.

Douglas fir, Colorado blue spruce, Scotch pine.

He didn't know which one Sarah would prefer, so after debating for several minutes, he chose a hearty Scotch pine and started the laborious process of chopping it down with an ax. It would have been much easier work if he'd had a chain saw. It was considerably more difficult than he expected, and he nearly took himself out when the tree fell. Still, he was pleased when he was able to trim up the branches and drag it back to the cabin. He could hardly wait to see everyone's excited expressions when he brought it in.

He smelled bacon even before he entered the cabin, heard the sizzle and snap of the meat cooking in an iron skillet. He hoped there'd be some fried eggs to go along with that bacon. Mmm.

"I fed the horses and the reindeer," he announced as he entered, shedding his coat and boots by the door and dragging the tree in behind him. Carl rushed to help him get the pine through the door.

Sarah was crouched before the fire, her gaze on the skillet, but when she heard Marcus's voice she stood and turned, wearing hot pads like mittens on both hands.

"Thank you. I wasn't looking forward to having to trek out in the freezing cold. You're just in time for—"

Her sentence slammed to a halt as she caught sight of his surprise and she gasped. All the color drained from her face.

His smile dropped from his lips. Why did he feel as if he'd just done something wrong? "I thought I'd bring everyone a little bit of Christmas cheer."

She pointed at the door, her jaw set with tension. "Get that thing out of here before—"

Before Onyx sees it.

But it was too late. Marcus's stomach tied into knots as Onyx rushed up to him, exclaiming in delight.

"A Christmas tree! It's Christmastime. I wish it could be Christmas every day."

Sarah's face went from white to cherry red. Marcus felt as if he was going to throw up. He still wasn't sure what he'd done wrong, but from Sarah's expression it was clear he'd made a horrible mistake, and he didn't know how to fix it. Onyx was already at his side, yanking on the trunk of the tree in a vain attempt to pull it farther into the house. He could hardly take it back now. Not without making the little girl cry.

His gaze moved from Onyx to Sarah. He didn't know what to do. Bring the tree in? Take it back out again? He couldn't just stand there in the doorway letting all the cold air in.

"Put the tree right over here, dear," Eliza instructed, pointing to the far corner of the living room. "This is where we put our tree every year. It's a tradition."

There was a small table up against the wall with a crocheted doily and some knickknacks on it, but Carl quickly moved it to another spot so it wouldn't be in the way when they put up the tree.

"I—er—okay," he stammered, pulling the pine to the corner Eliza had indicated.

"Looks like you've picked a good, stout tree there, son," Carl remarked, thumping Marcus on the back. "Nice choice, the Scotch pine. We've got a tree stand here somewhere. Eliza, where are all the Christmas decorations stored?"

"In the spare room closet, where we put them every year." Eliza rolled her eyes and everyone laughed.

Everyone except Sarah.

Marcus walked over to her and took her hand, drawing her aside so they could talk in relative privacy. "Sarah, I apologize. I didn't realize—"

"No," she said, cutting him off. "You *didn't* realize. You have no idea what you've just done."

He sighed deeply. She tried to remove her hand from his but he held it tight. "Tell me."

The sound that emerged from her throat could have passed for a growl. "I was trying so hard *not* to have to tell you this. It isn't your burden to carry."

"I didn't mean to upset you. Or Onyx."

"I know you didn't. But I'm not sure what I ought to do now. I thought Onyx wouldn't want to celebrate Christmas. Santa didn't come last year—and neither did her daddy."

"That's got to be hard for her. For all of you."

"It is." The color had drained from her face and she looked tired and sad. And maybe even a little ashamed as she said the next part, looking down and avoiding his eyes. "And the worst part is I projected my feelings onto Onyx. I assumed she wouldn't want a tree, decorations, presents. What an absurd thing to think. Of course she loves Christmas. She's a child. But now what am I going to do? I don't have a single thing for her. I didn't even shop for gifts."

Eliza approached, laying a hand on each of their shoulders. "I did. Now, Sarah, before you get upset about it, let me explain. I didn't want to say anything because I know how difficult this is for you, but Carl and I went shopping and we bought a few gifts for you and the girls. Just in case you changed your mind."

Tears sprang to Sarah's eyes. Just seeing her like this was ripping Marcus's heart into shreds. More than anything he wanted to make her smile again.

"Shall we bring out the decorations and trim the tree?" Eliza asked, patting Sarah on the shoulder. "It's your call, dear."

Marcus watched Sarah's expression as she glanced over at the corner where Onyx was "helping" her grandfather prop the tree up against the wall so they could place the trunk in the stand. Sarah pursed her lips and Marcus felt as much as saw the surge of emotion jolting through her.

At last she nodded and tried to chuckle, though it came out sounding strained. "That poor tree looks awfully bare. I guess we need to go help Onyx dress it up a bit."

"Perfect." Eliza clapped her hands. "Marcus, will you help me bring out the boxes of decorations?"

Boxes? Plural? For this small room?

"Yes, ma'am," he answered, gesturing for Eliza to go ahead of him down the hallway. "I'm at your service. Lead the way."

"Carl could learn some lessons in manners from you, young man," Eliza said over her shoulder, plenty loud enough for her husband to hear it.

Carl snorted. "Ho, ho, ho. Very funny, woman."

She giggled like a schoolgirl. Marcus could only hope he'd still be flirting with his wife when he got to be Carl and Eliza's age.

Wife? What wife?

When they reached the spare bedroom, Eliza pointed out the plastic bins she wanted him to pull out of the closet and haul back to the living room. Five in all. Most of them were lodged deep in the closet, and as he dived in to reach them, he noticed matching red suits lined with white fur hanging so far back in the closet that he wouldn't have seen them were he not digging for the bins.

He grabbed the hangers and held up the costumes so Eliza could see. "Mr. and Mrs. Claus, I presume."

She smiled and curtsied. "In the flesh. Or at least, we used to be, back when the farm was flourishing. Oh, how I miss those days. Carl just seemed to wither away after we hung up our costumes. He'd played Santa most of his adult life, you know. He loved working with all those children."

"If you don't mind me asking, what happened to the business? Why isn't the farm operational any longer?"

Eliza took his measure for a moment before answering. "You're going to have to ask Sarah for the details. Suffice it to say my son left us all in a world of hurt when he died, with a mountain of debt behind him that he'd hidden from us while he was alive. I believe he'd been trying to dig himself out of the mess before his accident, but his business acumen wasn't what it might have been. If only he'd shared his burden with us, we might have been able to help before things got that bad. Our outlook might be different.

"Sarah is the best daughter-in-love a mother could ask for and she's done everything in her power to save the farm as a legacy for her daughters, but it is just too great a burden for her. And I've shared too much already." She made a zipping motion over her lips.

Eliza's account explained so much—the run-down condition of the home and farm, the strain and stress that was so evident in Sarah's face, and why a frown appeared to come so much easier to her than a smile did.

He had so many more questions he wanted to ask, specific details that would help him determine how best to assist Sarah in climbing out of this hole, but he respected Eliza for backing off the subject. Sarah wouldn't want them discussing her private life behind her back.

"So these suits have been retired, then?"

Eliza sighed and nodded.

"Maybe we can have them make one last comeback? I'll bet Onyx would be delighted to have Santa and Mrs. Claus visit her in person on Christmas morning."

"What a lovely idea. I'm not sure how Sarah will feel about it, though."

"Don't worry about a thing. I'll ask her." He grinned and carefully laid the costumes on the bed, then turned to load up his arms with the plastic bins that held all the Christmas decorations.

"You and Sarah weren't friends in high school, were you?"

The question caught Marcus so far off guard that he stood abruptly and banged his head on the rim of the closet door.

"Ow," he muttered, rubbing his scalp. "That hurt."

He eyed Eliza, whose gaze glittered with amusement. "We were friends. All four years of high school. We graduated in the same class."

"No, what I meant to say is that you were *more* than friends, weren't you?"

"I—er—" he stammered. He started to deny it, but that would have been an outright lie. He blew out a breath. "Yes, ma'am, we were. We dated all the way through high school."

"I thought so. I've seen the way you look at her when you think no one is watching. She looks at you the same way, you know."

"She does?" That came as a surprise to him, more so than that Eliza was so quick on the uptake.

She nodded. She didn't look offended. Only curious. "If you don't mind my asking, what happened between you two?"

He shrugged. "Life, I guess, taking us on different paths. She was accepted into the School of Mines here in Colorado and I barely got into the state college in Oklahoma. My grades were never very good. I only squeaked by, while Sarah excelled. After I graduated, I went to work as a youth counselor at a therapy ranch in Texas and I've been there ever since. That's pretty much the whole story."

"You and Sarah didn't keep in touch?"

He shook his head. "I didn't know she was still in Colorado until she rode up to claim the reindeer blocking my truck."

"Well, I'm glad you're here, Marcus Ender. Sarah needs a reason to smile again."

The whole conversation could have been incredibly awkward, but somehow it wasn't. He liked Eliza Kendricks. He liked the whole family. And it made him feel incredibly blessed to be welcomed into their lives.

Marcus toted the bins out into the living room, and

after a simple lunch of peanut butter and jelly sandwiches, everyone spent the afternoon putting up decorations and trimming the tree. Eliza insisted on stringing lights even though the electricity was off.

"Just in case," she said.

The whole room was transformed into a wonderland of red and green. He'd never seen such a sight. It was so—*joyful*. Even Sarah appeared relaxed, her eyes sparkling with delight.

There was one last bin they hadn't yet opened. It was labeled as the crèche. Marcus called Onyx over to help him unpack the pieces. Together they lifted the lid. Marcus's heart thrummed in anticipation. The nativity was the center of Christmas and, as far as he was concerned, the very best part of putting up the decorations.

But when Onyx peeked inside the bin and spotted the ceramic figures, she didn't exclaim in delight as Marcus expected.

She burst into tears.

Sarah rushed to her sobbing daughter's side but Marcus was already there, patting Onyx's back and making unintelligible whispers of empathy. The little girl crawled into Marcus's arms and buried her head into his broad shoulder. Sarah wished she could do the same thing. She could use a little reassurance right now.

He met Sarah's gaze as she approached. "What did I do wrong?" he asked quietly, still rocking Onyx.

"It's not you," she assured him. "It's the nativity scene. I think she remembers how Justin made a big deal out of setting up the ceramic figures and reading the Bible story out of Luke. He let Onyx place the baby Jesus in the manger."

"Oh, wow." Marcus whistled under his breath. "Well, then. That's something."

He held Onyx away from him so he could look into her eyes. "We'll all pull out the figurines together," he told her. "We have Mary and Joseph, a shepherd with some sheep, a donkey, a camel and three wise men."

"And baby Jesus," Onyx added, wiping her wet cheeks with her palm.

"That's right, little darlin'. And you know, it's still your special responsibility to put Him in the manger where He belongs."

"It is?" Onyx sniffled.

"You bet it is. We all depend on you."

"I've got my Bible right here," Carl said, holding up a dog-eared leather-bound volume. "The nativity is one story that never gets old."

"Marcus, will you do the honors?" Sarah asked. It wasn't that he took the place of Justin. But Sarah found her heart expanding. There was room for Marcus. Maybe there always had been.

"Absolutely not," he replied. He took her hand and led her to the easy chair. "That honor belongs to you."

He removed Jewel from her arms so Onyx could crawl into her lap. Carl and Eliza sat on the sofa, and as Sarah read the blessed story, they all placed the figurines on the coffee table. Marcus stood by the side of the armchair, bouncing from foot to foot and rubbing Jewel's back to keep her happy.

Sarah got so choked up when she reached the birth of Jesus that she could barely read. Her eyes pricked with tears as Onyx proudly yet meekly placed the baby in the manger.

This time Sarah allowed her tears to fall. She felt as

if she'd been washed clean, her spirit lightened as her burdens slipped away. In the big scheme of things her problems didn't seem so enormous. In fact, they were rather miniscule.

This was exactly what she needed—the reminder that God loved her enough to send His Son to earth, to become a human like her. Both Jesus and Mary knew what it was to experience joy and sorrow. To know love and suffer loss.

Suddenly she didn't feel so alone.

Marcus laid his hand on her shoulder, almost as if he sensed what this moment meant to her. She glanced up and met his warm gaze and then covered his hand with hers.

Everyone was silent for a moment as they viewed the crèche through the flickering glow of the fire, and then Carl and Eliza burst into applause. Sarah and Marcus joined in and Onyx dropped into a cute little curtsy.

"Where'd she learn how to do that?" Marcus asked.

"I have no idea."

He shook his head. "She just stole my heart clean away."

And Marcus had just stolen Sarah's.

They ate hot dogs for the second night in a row and finished the meal off with another batch of s'mores. No one complained. Cooking food over an open fire was still a novelty.

"Who's up for some Christmas carols?" Eliza asked as soon as supper was finished. She slid onto the bench behind the old upright piano and ran her fingers across the keys. Sarah thought it might be a little out of tune. The piano had belonged to Eliza's mother, and Sarah hadn't had the heart to sell it with the rest of their furniture.

Marcus helped Sarah to her feet from where she was

sitting cross-legged near the fire, but he didn't let go of her hand even when she was standing on her own volition. Instead, he led her over next to the piano and linked his fingers with hers.

If Carl or Eliza noticed, they didn't say anything, and though Sarah imagined in any other circumstance she might have felt awkward, it somehow seemed right for Marcus to be sharing Christmas Eve with her. With the family.

"Just so you know," Marcus said with a chuckle, "I'm as tone-deaf as one of those goats you've seen videos of online."

"It's your heart that counts, son, not your voice."

Marcus exaggerated a wince. "You say that now."

Eliza jumped into a lively rendition of "Jingle Bells" and everyone joined in. Onyx sat on the bench next to her grandmother and belted out the tune in her sweet little voice, her excitement growing with every refrain.

She hit more right notes than Marcus did. He hadn't overstated his lack of musical expertise. The man missed more notes than he hit, but his enthusiasm more than made up for his deficiencies. As they moved on to more traditional Christmas hymns, he sang with such reverence and awe that she couldn't fault him a single note, even if they weren't exactly what was written in the hymnal.

By the time they finished the evening with a soft, slow rendition of "Silent Night," both of the children were asleep. Jewel was tucked into the porta-crib and Onyx was curled up on the floor next to the piano, wrapped in her blankie with Brownie tucked under her chin.

Carl exaggerated a yawn. "Eliza and I had better hit the hay."

"So should we," Sarah agreed, although she didn't really want the night to end. If she had her way it would last forever. Being part of something bigger than herself. Rejoicing in the joy of the real reason for the season.

"Not yet, you don't." Carl belted out a laugh that sounded suspiciously like Santa Claus. "You two have been standing there all evening and you never even noticed what was hanging right over your heads." He pointed to a spot on the ceiling.

Sarah and Marcus looked up simultaneously.

Mistletoe. What crazy person had hung a sprig of mistletoe right in the middle of the room?

Carl grinned, looking smug.

"Oh, go on, son," Eliza said, gesturing to Marcus. "Carl's not going to let you off the hook until the deed is done. You might as well get it over with."

Sarah felt as if all the air had left the room. She gasped for breath but oxygen eluded her. Her head started spinning. When Marcus reached for her shoulders and turned her toward him, she was certain she was going to lose consciousness. Her legs felt weak and gooey, and when Marcus smiled sheepishly, her stomach fluttered as if an entire kaleidoscope of butterflies had been let loose.

Marcus's blue eyes glittered and the fire made his hair shine like spun gold. When he slid his palm from her shoulders to frame her face, she forgot they had an audience.

They were the only two people in the room. The only two people on the planet.

He smiled his amazing half smile, and his gaze dropped to her lips. She wondered if he could feel her quivering. She thought he might be, too.

It seemed like forever before he finally leaned down and gently brushed his lips against hers. So soft. So dear. So sweet.

The *audience* applauded.

Marcus bowed. And the moment shattered like a rock through a mirror.

"Did you ask her yet?" Eliza directed her question to Marcus.

"Ask me what?" She stiffened.

"I haven't had the opportunity. We've been pretty busy all day." He slid his arm around her shoulders and gave her a squeeze. He was buttering her up for something.

"What do you want?"

"We were thinking that it might be a fun idea if Santa and Mrs. Claus made an appearance tomorrow morning. Do you think Onyx would like that?"

She looked from an eager Marcus, who sounded almost childlike in his enthusiasm, to Carl and Eliza. Their faces were lit up as brightly as the flames in the fire. She hadn't realized just how important those roles were to them. Now that the Christmas tree farm was being torn from her grasp, she would have nothing to offer them.

Her heart dropped into her stomach, but she forced her lips into a smile that she wasn't feeling. "Of course. What a great idea. I'm sure Onyx would love it."

"Awesome!" Marcus did a little victory dance. "No Heat Miser or Snow Miser this year. Not another year without a Santa Claus."

Sarah gasped and her jaw dropped. Heat rose to her face and her hands trembled.

"I—I—" she stammered, and then burst into tears.

Chapter Six

Could he possibly have been any less sensitive?

Marcus wanted to kick himself into next Tuesday. He'd gone and said the most hurtful thing ever, reminding everyone in this beautiful family of all they had lost. Sarah most of all.

"Oh, darlin', I'm sorry." He tried to wrap his arms around her but she wrested out of his reach. She wouldn't even look him in the eye.

He winced and turned to apologize to Carl and Eliza for his thoughtless comment, but Carl was already guiding Eliza toward the hideaway. Their eyes met and Marcus opened his mouth to speak, but Carl shook his head. The message was clear.

Marcus had done enough damage for one night.

Sarah stared blankly out the front window, hugging herself against the chill—or against tactless statements made by foolish men.

He walked up behind her, everything in him urging him to touch her, to wrap his arms around her and never let her go. But he was afraid that might be the worst thing he could do, so he gritted his teeth and shoved his hands into the front pockets of his jeans.

He didn't know what to say so he remained silent. Their gazes met in the reflection of the window.

"The storm is finally letting up," she said, her voice a monotone. "You should be able to leave tomorrow. I hate that you have to travel on Christmas Day, but—"

So that was it, then. She wanted him to go. She'd dropped the end of her sentence, but her meaning was clear enough. He was no longer welcome in her house. He could hardly blame her for feeling that way, but it still broke his heart.

"I'm not mad at you," she whispered, turning so suddenly that she stepped right into his personal space, close enough for him to smell the sweet apple scent of her shampoo. Close enough for their breaths to mingle.

"You should be," he ground out.

"No. I shouldn't. You brought Christmas back into our home, and for that I am grateful. I never should have pushed it out of our lives—you showed me that. The truth is, I've been struggling with circumstances beyond my control lately and I hate that I don't know what to do about them."

He could relate. He still had no idea how he was going to respond to his mother's sudden reappearance in his life. But they were talking about Sarah.

"Eliza told me a little bit." He brushed a stray lock of hair behind her ear.

"Did she tell you we're losing the farm?"

"What? No. She said Justin left some debt but—"

"The bank is threatening foreclosure and I have no way to stop it. I have no idea where we'll all end up. I sold most of our household goods and business fixtures, and I used up my entire savings, but it just wasn't enough."

No wonder there were dark circles under her eyes. She'd not only single-handedly taken on the responsibility of the floundering Christmas tree farm, but all of its residents.

She sighed. "It was supposed to be my children's legacy." She laid her palm on his chest, over his heart. He wondered if she could feel how hard it was pounding, and with such an irregular rhythm. "But at least you're taking the Percherons with you. I can find consolation in that. Sheryl will be good to them."

He hadn't planned on *taking* the Percherons. But now how could he not? The way she spoke of it, he'd be relieving her of a burden. Animals that size probably cost a pretty penny in upkeep.

"I've been angry at God for a long time," she admitted softly.

"I understand," he murmured. "I think everyone gets angry with God at least once in their walk with Him, when circumstances appear beyond their control. We can't always see the big picture, I guess."

Even as he spoke the words, he was turning them back on himself.

"Like with your mother, you mean?"

"Exactly. But then I think what happens is that we enter a vicious cycle—we're angry with God, and then we get frustrated with ourselves for having so little faith."

Her eyes brightened, shining with fresh, unshed tears. He wrapped his arms around her waist and pulled her into a hug. He hadn't meant to make her cry again.

"And through it all, He loves us unconditionally." Her voice was muffled by the fabric of his shirt.

"See? You're not just beautiful. You're smart, too." There he went again, back to cracking jokes when his emotions got too uncomfortable for him to handle. When would he learn to just shut up?

Her shoulders quivered. Great. He'd gone and made her start bawling again. He felt like an utter oaf.

But when she leaned back and looked into his eyes, he realized she wasn't crying at all.

She was laughing.

And he'd never seen anything more welcome. The storm outside was nothing compared to the one going on in his chest.

He didn't want to leave tomorrow. He didn't want to leave *ever*. There was a reason he'd never been able to form a solid long-term relationship with a woman, and it wasn't because of his mother, as he'd once believed.

No, it was because of the woman in his arms, a woman who'd had the courage to expose her faith— and her heart—to him, even though she knew he was going to walk away.

His heart hammered in his chest as she wrapped her arms around his neck and stood on tiptoe so her lips could find his. He bent his head and deepened the kiss, expressing everything he wanted to say. He had no words, but he had this.

He was in love with her. Maybe he always had been.

From what seemed like a great distance, Marcus heard a click and then the lights on the Christmas tree flickered and came to life, dancing to the tune of his heart. And along with that came the painful reminder that it was nearly time for him to go home.

* * *

Sarah stayed awake long after Marcus dozed off in the chair. It was so late by the time the electricity turned on that they'd decided to stay in the living room for one more night.

His kiss had changed her world. She loved Marcus more than she thought it was possible to love a man. Just as she had when she was eighteen, and had run away from the strength of her feelings for him, looking for something more "practical" that wouldn't overwhelm her. She might even love him more now. She ached with it, thought her heart might burst like fireworks at midnight on New Year's Eve.

But there would be no new year for them. There would be no new anything. He was leaving in the morning, going back to celebrate the holidays with his family, then back to working with the youth in Texas.

She had no part in that. She had a family to worry about. She still had to find them a place to live and a way to sustain them after she had to give up the farm.

With the electricity came heat and the cabin soon warmed. Sarah watched the fire die down to glowing embers before she hung the stockings on the mantel. She'd crocheted mittens and scarves for everyone. She had made extra for the church closet and picked out a set she thought Marcus might like, as well. She found an extra stocking at the bottom of one of the bins and doctored it up with some glitter and glue. At least she could give him something to remember her by.

Finally, physically and emotionally worn out, she curled up next to Onyx and fell into an uneasy sleep.

She awoke to a hearty "Ho, ho, ho" and the feeling that she was being bounced up and down on a balloon.

She cracked one eye open. Onyx was jumping on the air mattress, clapping her hands in delight.

Well, that explained the bouncy feeling.

"Wake up, Mama. Wake up. Santa is here."

She groaned and rolled over. She was *so* not ready for this day to begin. Marcus was leaving.

Presents had been wrapped and scattered under the tree—Eliza and Carl must have put them out at some point this morning. Carl was trussed up in his red suit. Eliza had even dabbed his cheeks with rouge. She was by his side, laughing at Onyx's reaction to their costumes.

"Have you been a good girl this year?" Carl sat down in the armchair and gestured to Onyx to sit on his lap.

Where was Marcus? The last Sarah had seen of him, he'd been dozing in that very armchair. Her adrenaline rocketed and her pulse beat overtime. Had he already left?

No. He couldn't have gone. Not without saying goodbye.

She sat up abruptly, scanning the room for the golden-haired man with the knockout smile.

"The little lady happens to be a princess. If ever a girl deserved a gift from Santa, it's Onyx Kendricks."

Marcus entered the living room from the kitchen, carrying two mugs of steaming coffee. He grinned and headed straight for her.

"I thought you might need a little caffeine boost, considering the late night you had."

Relief flooded through her. She was glad she was still sitting down or she might have fallen. She was so taken in by his smile that she just wanted to pull him to her and kiss him until he promised to stay.

But there were others in the room and she couldn't possibly ask him to stay anyway, so instead she reached for the coffee and took a long, fortifying sip of the hot liquid. "How do you know I was up late?"

He nodded toward the mantel, where the stocking with his name written in dabs of glitter glue hung with the others. "Apparently Onyx wasn't the only one Santa visited."

"I hope you like what I made for you. I didn't have time to put much together."

He knit his eyebrows. "I feel bad. I don't have anything for you."

She brushed her palm against the scruff on his cheek. "You've done too much already. Your presence is more than enough of a gift for me, and I know my family feels the same way."

"Sarah, I—" he started, but he didn't get a chance to continue his thought.

Carl interrupted him, loudly clearing his throat. "There's a little girl here who is getting impatient for her present."

Marcus crouched by Sarah and turned so he could see Onyx.

Carl's belly really shook when he laughed, just like that bowl full of jelly. He reached into his sack and produced Onyx's gift with a flourish.

"My dolly!"

Sarah groaned under her breath. "Yep. That's the one."

Onyx hugged the doll and it cried out with an obnoxious "A-wah, a-wah."

Marcus chuckled and leaned close to her ear. "I still think it's creepy. Good luck with that."

"I already have one fussy baby," she said as Jewel awoke and made her presence known.

"Now we both have a baby, don't we, Mama?"

Sarah picked up Jewel and embraced Onyx. "We sure do, sweetheart. Now, why don't you go give Santa a kiss on his cheek so he can be on his way? I'm sure he has many more children to visit this Christmas."

Santa and Mrs. Claus made a quick exit and Carl and Eliza appeared a few minutes later, their wide smiles telling Sarah how much they'd enjoyed the morning, far more than they could with words.

Sarah took the stockings off the mantel and passed them out as they all gathered around the tree. Carl and Eliza had bought her favorite perfume and some bubble bath. She sat cross-legged and fed Jewel a bottle while the rest of the family dug into their stockings. Everyone seemed to like the scarves and mittens she'd crocheted for them.

Onyx promptly wrapped her scarf around her new doll and "fed" her with the tiny bottle that had accompanied the toy.

"Just like her mama," Marcus said with a wink. He took his own scarf and swung it over his shoulder in an overexaggerated fashion model movement. He shoved his hands into his new mittens and struck a pose.

"What do you think? I could be a model, right?"

Sarah's breath caught in her throat. He could definitely be a model with that golden hair and lady-killer smile.

He removed his mittens and crouched in front of her, brushing his palm over Jewel's dark curls. "Thank you again, darlin'. I wish I had something for you."

"You gave me something priceless."

His brow rose. "I did?"

"Christmas."

His gaze locked with hers for a long moment and the

warmth she read there almost convinced her that he was going to change his mind and stay with her.

An incoherent sound emerged from the back of his throat and he rocked back on his heels.

"I should go," he said hoarsely.

Stay.

She wanted to throw herself into his arms, beg him not to leave. But for his sake, she did the hardest thing she'd ever had to do in her life.

She broke eye contact and looked away.

"I was going to ask you to stick around and bake cookies with us, but I imagine your family is eagerly awaiting your presence at your grandma's house."

He chuckled, but it sounded forced. "I don't know how *eager* Matt is to see me, but you're right. I'd better load up the Percherons and be on my way."

She clutched Jewel to her shoulder and rocked her, doing her best to stem the tears that had sprung to her eyes. Marcus put on his coat and boots and reached for his hat. He opened the door to leave and then seemed to think better of it. He turned and crossed the room in three large strides and then crouched before her.

His expression was unreadable as he leaned forward and brushed his lips across her cheek.

"Goodbye, Sarah," he whispered. "I'll be praying for you."

She tried to return the sentiment, to let him know she'd be praying for him and the situation with his mother, but her throat closed around the words. She nodded and squeezed her eyes shut against the tears that were threatening to fall.

When she pulled herself together enough to open her eyes, Marcus was gone.

Chapter Seven

Marcus had the Percherons loaded up in the trailer and had made it as far as the cab in his truck before he realized what an idiot he was being.

He couldn't take Sarah's horses away from her, the last vestiges of her life on the farm. Well, except for Snort and Crash. The two reindeer had sounded like a whole pen full of pigs when he'd gone to load the horses. They clearly weren't happy with him for taking away their stablemates.

He couldn't leave this way.

He couldn't leave at *all*.

He was in love with Sarah, and no matter what the future offered, his place was by her side. If she'd let him, it would be his privilege to help her raise Onyx and Jewel, and maybe even add a baby brother or sister or two if they were so blessed. He loved Sarah's daughters already and looked forward to watching them grow.

If she'd let him, he'd also help her save the farm. He had years of unused salary tucked away. He lived a simple life on a ranch with his room and board covered. He didn't have any reason to spend the money he received in salary.

He'd gratefully give every penny to Sarah. Along with Carl and Eliza, they could rebuild the farm and make it into the thriving business he knew it could be.

They'd take guests into the forest on the sleigh to pick out their special trees. Mag and Jes would be a team again. Happy children would visit with Santa, and the silly reindeer would even get to play their part. Maybe they'd open a gift shop with one-of-a-kind gifts and ornaments. Sarah could even sell some of her scarves if she was so inclined. Excitement built in his chest just thinking about the possibilities.

It could happen. Together, they could make it happen.

But he was getting ahead of himself.

Way, *way* ahead of himself.

He hadn't even spoken to Sarah about how he felt about her, never mind asking her how she felt about him. The kiss they'd shared the night before had rocked his world. Had it meant as much to her as it had to him?

He needed to unload the horses before he could go back to the house and get the answers to his questions, but first he decided to call Grandma Sheryl. She and Matt were probably worried about him, and he couldn't wait to share the news that he was staying with Sarah.

If he was staying with Sarah.

It might be presumptuous of him, but he was already planning how to give his notice to Redemption Ranch and find an apartment nearby so he could help get the farm back in working order.

Thankfully, cell phone reception had been restored. To Marcus's surprise, Matt answered the phone. Even more astonishing, his brother seemed to have mellowed out with age, or at least he had matured. Apparently there was a woman in the picture, and Marcus was happy for him.

In all the excitement, Marcus *may* have jumped the gun and declared his feelings for Sarah, but he couldn't seem to help himself. He was just so happy. He even felt comfortable enough to tell Matt about their mother calling. When he told Matt that he was ready to let the resentment go, his brother shocked him by saying he was proud of him. Marcus hadn't realized how badly he'd wanted to hear that until the words were said.

Matt passed the phone to Grandma Sheryl. She was laughing as she answered.

"Marcus?" she said. "I've been praying for you. We were worried about you. When you didn't arrive on time, we checked the weather and realized a storm had probably hit where you were. We prayed you were safe and warm."

"Yeah, sorry about that. There was no reception up at Sarah's farm after the storm set in."

"I figured as much. Are you on your way now?"

"No. That's what I wanted to talk to you about." He paused, expecting Grandma to be surprised, or at least startled.

"Things went well, I take it?"

"I'm afraid to ask you what you mean by that."

"Why don't you tell me?"

"I was stranded at Sarah's cabin. Carl and Eliza were there, along with the girls. We lost power. We had to work together to stay warm and make Christmas happen, but we managed to figure it out."

"Meaning?"

He took a deep breath and dived in. "I'm in love with

Sarah. I'm not sure if I ever fell out of love with her, but you already know that, don't you? I'm going to ask her to be my wife."

"Let me be the first to congratulate you—well, second, if you count Matt."

"About the horses," Marcus started, not quite sure how to approach the subject. "I'd like to buy them back from you. I'm hoping Sarah will agree not only to marry me, but to give this farm another go. And she really loves the Percherons."

"Consider them a wedding gift. I don't know what I'd do with a couple of draft horses, anyway."

"They why did you—?"

"You know Sarah. She's a proud woman. She wouldn't take charity, but I wanted to find some way to help her. That's why I sent you. I knew the Lord would work it all out in His own good timing."

"You figured it out long before I did," Marcus admitted. "I must be the thickest man alive. I almost drove out of here without telling Sarah how I feel."

"But you didn't."

"No. I didn't. But I haven't actually spoken to Sarah about my intentions yet. I don't even know if she'll accept me."

"She will," Grandma said definitively. "Now scoot and go ask that woman to be your wife."

"Yes, ma'am. I will." He paused. He didn't want to ruin the moment, but the truth had to be spoken. "I have more to tell you. About Mom. She called me."

"I know. She called me, as well."

Even though Grandma couldn't see him, Marcus gaped in surprise. "She did?"

"Yes, and I know how difficult this will be for you

and Matt. All I can say is, we'll figure it out as a family, okay?"

As a family. He liked the sound of that.

"All right." Marcus felt as if a load had been taken off his shoulders. "Merry Christmas, Grandma. I love you."

"Merry Christmas, sweetheart. I love you, too."

Marcus ended the call and then leaned back and closed his eyes, blowing out a breath to steady his nerves. Now came the hard part.

It was now or never. If he waited much longer he would start to freeze up like an icicle. Fortunately, unloading the horses was faster than loading them and it wasn't long before Mag and Jes were happily ensconced in their stalls with fresh hay and a bucket of oats. Even the reindeer appeared to be content.

"I guess I have you to thank for this," he told Crash as he passed her stall. "I'll give you an extra handful of oats for your effort."

Crash pricked her ears forward and snuffed at him as if she understood what he was saying.

He was laughing as he exited the stable and made his way up to the cabin, but by the time he reached the front door his breath was coming in painfully short gasps and a line of sweat dotted his brow, as if he'd run miles to get here.

In a way, he supposed, he had.

He unlatched the gold chain he always wore around his neck and slid the ring he'd worn next to his heart all these years into the palm of his hand. Removing his hat, he swiped his forearm across his brow and took another deep breath.

Now or never. He rang the bell.

Sarah's eyes widened in surprise when she opened the door, Jewel propped on her hip.

Eliza appeared next to her, giving Marcus a quick once-over before she took Jewel from Sarah's arms. "I'll put her down for a nap for you, dear."

Sarah nodded absently and then, as if remembering herself, stood back and gestured Marcus inside. The usually bustling living room was noticeably void of people, elderly or preschool-aged.

"Is something wrong?" Sarah asked.

Marcus rolled the brim of his hat in his fists. He'd never been so nervous in his life. "No. Yes." He shook his head. "Not wrong, exactly, but—"

"Is it one of the horses?" Concern laced her tone.

"No. Mag and Jes are in their stalls. I fed them some fresh oats. The reindeer, too."

"I don't understand. I thought you'd have taken the horses and would have been long gone by now."

"That's just it. I can't leave, Sarah. Not without telling you how much I love you."

From the look on her face, he wasn't sure he should have blurted his feelings out quite the way he had, but he was already all-in, so he rushed onward. "I know we've only had a couple of days together since we reconnected, but I know how I feel, and that's not going to change."

She started to speak but he jumped in, afraid she might reject him out of hand, just as she'd done when they were teenagers.

"I don't mean to pressure you, and I don't care how long I have to wait for you to return my feelings. My heart is yours. Oh—and I forgot to give you your Christmas gift."

He opened his hand and held up the shiny gold ring. The solitaire sapphire glinted in the sunlight. "I've had this for a long time. Since high school, actually."

"Since *high school*?" she exclaimed.

"A few days before you broke up with me, to be precise. I'd planned to give you this ring, to pledge my heart to you."

She gasped and covered her mouth with her palm. "I had no idea your feelings ran so deep."

"Neither did I. Not until I met you again a couple of days ago and realized the reason I still wore this ring on a chain around my neck wasn't because I was sappy or sentimental, although I'm probably both, but because I never stopped loving you. If you'll let me, I'll spend the rest of my life trying to make you happy. Onyx and Jewel, too."

She launched herself into his arms, squeezing his neck so tightly that he couldn't breathe. That was okay. He wasn't sure his lungs were working, anyway. His heart had expanded so much he doubted there was room in his chest for anything else.

"My heart broke in two when you left this morning," she admitted. "I wanted to run after you and tell you to stay."

He leaned back so he could look into her eyes. "Why didn't you?"

"Do you realize what you're committing yourself to? I come with so much baggage it isn't even funny."

"Well, the way I see it, your kids are definitely benefits, and I've grown very fond of Carl and Eliza."

"But in the rest of my life I'm tanking big-time. The farm—"

"—can be saved," he finished for her. He grinned

and kissed her cheek. "I'm sure the bank is closed for the holidays, but we'll be first in line to pay off the debt on the farm come the first of the year."

"But how?"

"I've got money. Loads of it. I think God had me planning for this moment even before I could conceive of it. We can sit down and make up a new business plan and bring this Christmas tree farm back to life."

"You really believe we can?"

"I do."

Hope flashed in her eyes but then she frowned. "I can't ask you to do that."

"You're not asking, darlin'. I'm offering. And I'm not taking no for an answer." He paused, considering. "That is, unless you don't want me in your life."

"You think I don't want you in my life? Are you crazy?"

He shrugged, trying and failing to keep his smile under wraps. "Possibly. Though if it helps my case, I think I might have an in with your horses. And I know the reindeer like me."

"Mr. Marcus!" Onyx raced into the room and threw herself on his leg. "You're back."

He raised his eyebrows at Sarah. "Am I?"

Her smile would have lit up the room even if the electricity had still been out. "Apparently the children like you, too."

He winked at her and ruffled Onyx's dark curls. "Yes, little darlin'," he said. "It appears I'm back for good."

"You're *home*," Sarah whispered, wrapping her arms around his waist and resting her head on his shoulder.

He reached for her left hand and slid the ring on her finger. His heart raced as she paused to admire it.

He bent his head so he could speak in her ear. "It's

only a promise ring." He kissed her temple. "But I *promise* I'm going to replace it with an engagement ring, and then a wedding ring. The sooner, the better."

"I'm going to hold you to that, cowboy."

"I'd be disappointed if you didn't." He chuckled and hugged her tight. "And so would the reindeer."

* * * * *

Dear Reader,

Marcus Ender has been lurking around Redemption Ranch in Serendipity, Texas, for several stories now, patiently waiting for his own happily-ever-after. In *The Cowboy's Yuletide Reunion*, Marcus travels to Colorado on an errand for his grandmother, only to encounter the woman he once loved. With her children and in-laws, Marcus and Sarah learn to forgive, trust and love again.

Christmas is a wonderful time to pause and remember all God has done for us in sending His Son to be born of a virgin in a humble stable in Bethlehem. Jesus experienced joy and sorrow just as we do. Even when things are at their darkest, God shines His light into our souls. Let us rejoice with the angels, wise men and shepherds as we celebrate the season of Christ's birth.

I wish you, my reader, a merry Christmas and a very happy New Year. I love to connect with you in a personal way. You can look me up at http://www.debkastnerbooks.com. Come visit me on Facebook at http://www.facebook.com/debkastnerbooks, or you can catch me on Twitter @debkastner.

Please know that you are daily in my prayers. I appreciate you more than words can say.

Love Courageously,

Deb Kastner

THE COWBOY'S CHRISTMAS GIFT

Arlene James

Two are better than one,
because they have a good reward for their toil.
—*Ecclesiastes* 4:9

Chapter One

The Christmas lights along Main Street twinkled merrily as Matthew Ender drove his sweet new double-cab pickup truck through the small town of Red Bluff, Oklahoma. The hour had gone well past midnight, making it technically the second of December. In a just world, he'd have been in Las Vegas participating in the Professional Rodeo Cowboys Association National Finals Rodeo. Instead, he'd spent the past week in a hospital in Florida, having the ligaments, muscle and skin surgically restored to the thumb of his right hand, which throbbed just now with a power that made his whole body hurt.

He'd only meant to solidify his place in the finals with one last win in Florida and pick up some extra cash, but he'd been riding a horse in training, and the critter had sidestepped at just the wrong moment. Matt's hand had gotten caught in the dally, the wrap of his rope around the saddle horn, while he was in the process of dismounting. When the horse had sidestepped, it had taken the glove off his hand and all the meat and sinew right off his thumb with it, leaving the bare bone exposed.

A good sports doctor on site had stopped the bleeding and rescued the tissue, but Matt's first trip to the National Finals in his nearly eleven-year-long rodeo career had ended before it had even begun, and he'd spent a good chunk of his year's earnings paying the hospital bills. He'd had no real choice but to head back home to his grandmother's ranch, where he'd grown up, in order to recuperate.

Well, at least Grandma Sheryl would finally get her wish to have both her grandsons home for Christmas. Usually only Matt's younger brother, Marcus, showed up. It had been so long since Matt had come home that Sheryl would probably faint at the sight of him. She'd have to faint in the morning, though. He was too tired and in too much pain to deal with a homecoming tonight. Driving himself had meant staying off the pain meds, and twenty-four straight hours of that had just about killed him.

Matt had done some serious praying since that horse had sidestepped. He hadn't done much of that in the years after his dad had died in a tractor accident when he was thirteen, but time had knocked some sense into him, and after he'd talked to the doctors about his thumb, he'd prayed almost without ceasing. He'd prayed first just to keep his thumb, then to be able to rope and ride again. Now he prayed to make it home in one piece. Hurting now and so tired he could barely see, he prayed himself out of town and over those familiar old country roads.

He'd been home every now and then over the years, for an hour or two here and there, just to check on Gran and see that the old place was still standing. Strangely, though, as he'd done better and better, he'd found less and less time to come by, and never at Christmas. Those Christmases after his dad died had always been dreary, miserable times for Matt. He didn't figure his presence now would really bring any joy to anyone, but for Grandma's sake, he'd try to get into the spirit of the holiday.

When he reached the turn-in, he saw that the old Ender's Ranch sign over the drive was down. He wondered how long ago that had happened. It had been a couple of years since he'd last made this trip, but Gran hadn't said anything about needing a new sign during their infrequent phone calls. He eased the truck over the cattle guard and aimed it down the sandy road.

When the truck topped that next little rise, the house came into view. It looked weathered, in need of a good coat of white paint. The steep roof that sloped down from the second story to shelter the porch, which fanned out on two sides, gleamed new in the moonlight, though, as it was made of durable metal. A scrawny scrub cedar had grown up at the corner of the porch. Gran had decorated it for Christmas with fuzzy ropes of tinsel and a tinfoil star. It looked like something he and his brother, Marcus, would have done back when they were kids and Christmas had still been the most exciting time of the year.

He parked under the old hickory tree and hauled himself out of the cab, taking the keys but leaving his coat and bags in the truck. A little old sedan sat at the side of the house where the kitchen door opened onto the porch. Apparently Grandma had taken to driving a car instead of a truck. The car would be cheaper to operate, yet, if Matt wasn't mistaken, that was a shiny new horse trailer he saw sitting in the barn out back there. She must be storing it for somebody. Folks around here did that for each other. The barn looked in good repair. It was too dark to see beyond it to the corral.

Too tired to give matters much more thought, he held his injured right hand up by the wrist, his left hand clamped around it, and walked to the front door, praying his key still worked. The key turned, but he struggled to unlock the door with his left hand. After he got it open, he quietly closed and locked the door then sat down in the old rocker to pull off his boots. He didn't want to wake Gran; he just wanted to swallow his pain pills and get to bed.

Fishing the prescription bottle out of his shirt pocket with a finger, he climbed the stairs. Moonlight fell from the window at the top of the landing, but memory guided his tired feet more than sight. Turning left, he popped the top off the bottle and shook two capsules into his mouth then swallowed them gratefully before tucking away the bottle. Meanwhile, he made his way along the landing to the hallway that divided the upstairs into two equal parts. It consisted of just four rooms, two on each side—three bedrooms and one bath.

Gran had the front room on the left, with the bathroom behind. His dad had claimed the front room on the right, and Matt and his brother had shared the second room at the back until their father had died. Then Matt had reluctantly moved into his dad's room. He went there, hating the feel, even now, of taking his father's place and at the same time anxious to fall into bed.

After slowly opening the door for fear it might squeak on its hinges—no telling when it had been opened last—he walked across the room on his stocking feet to the bed, which was thankfully where he'd left it. Then he simply let himself collapse onto the mattress.

It wasn't a mattress he fell onto, however, but another warm body, which immediately began to screech and scramble, knocking against his bandaged hand in the process. He roared in pain, tumbling onto the floor.

"Get out! Get out! Get out!" a woman screamed. A *young* woman—definitely not his grandma.

Confused, he shouted back. "Be quiet!" At the same time, he tried to leverage himself up in the dark without using his right hand.

"I mean it! Get out of here! I'm armed!"

"I don't care," he growled, figuring that if she were going to shoot him, she already would have. "What are you doing in my bed?"

"*Your* bed?" she screeched just as the overhead light flashed on.

Grandma Sheryl stood in the doorway, her short, silver hair standing on end, her wrapper askew. What made Matt's jaw drop, though, was the beautiful woman the light showed him at the foot of the bed. Short and curvy, judging by the fit of her sweats, with long, straight, light red hair, she wielded his old baseball bat, murder in her big, clear blue eyes.

"Matthew Ender," Sheryl demanded, "what on earth are you doing here?"

Well, *that* wasn't exactly the welcome home he'd been expecting. He frowned at her over the thick bandage on his injured hand. "Merry Christmas to you, too, Gran."

"Get up from there," she said, coming forward to help him to his feet. She seemed to have shrunk since he'd seen her last, and he noticed a few more wrinkles, but she looked to be in good shape. She sniffed at him as he struggled up. "Have you been drinking?"

"No! You know I don't drink. I just drove in from Florida."

She put a hand to her back as if helping him up had strained her. "Thought you'd be in Las Vegas."

"Would've been, if I hadn't hurt myself in Florida," he muttered. He shot his chin at the beauty, who had let the bat slide through her hands to rest on the floor. "Who's this sleeping in my bed?"

"*My* bed," she corrected smartly.

"This is my partner, Neely Spence."

Matt frowned. That name sounded familiar, but with the shock of the past few minutes, the pain still hammering at him, and the medication starting to swirl through his system, he couldn't concentrate on more than one thought at a time. "Partner? What do you need a partner for?"

"Never you mind," Grandma said. "We've got to make some adjustments. Neely, honey, could you sleep in with Amber for the time being?"

"Amber?" Matt parroted, starting to feel decidedly light-headed. He dropped down onto the side of the bed. "Who's Amber?"

"My baby sister," Neely said, glaring a warning at him as she snatched a pink pillow from the bed, *his* bed.

"My baby sister," he mimicked in a tiny voice, watching as she swept from the room, pillow in one hand, bat in the other. Well, that explained the cedar tree out front.

"You are a scoundrel, Matthew Ender," Gran said affectionately. "What did you do to your hand?"

He held up the throbbing appendage. "De-gloved the index finger." It was an injury all ropers feared.

She made a face. "Yow. Must've hurt like the dickens."

"Worse."

She came over and kissed him on the forehead. "I'm glad you came home. Need anything?"

"Sleep."

Pushing on his shoulders, she made him lie back, then emptied his pockets. After lifting his legs onto the bed, she pulled the covers from beneath him and tucked them around him, clucking her tongue as he pulled his bandaged hand free. He might have been ten years old again. It made him feel warm and loved.

"Thanks, Grandma."

"We'll talk tomorrow," she said, rubbing the hair on top of his head the way his dad had always done. "Sleep now."

"Mmm." He sighed, halfway to dreamland. His last conscious thought was that Neely Spence was mighty pretty, but he needed to know who she was and why she'd moved in on his grandma.

The bright December sun had moved well over the east-facing windows of the house and hung very near the apex of the roofline by the time Neely spotted the dust cloud rolling up from the paved road. Company was coming. Make that *more* company. Although he was technically family, she couldn't think of Sheryl's grandson Matt as anything else. He certainly hadn't been around to help his grandma with this place in years. He had some gall even calling it "home" after the way he'd all but abandoned his grandmother. She knew his kind. He'd heal up and head out. That's what these rodeo bums did. She'd seen enough of them during her barrel-racing career to know.

After pushing her hat back to take another look at that dust cloud, she backed the showy butternut bay quarter horse into the starting stall and climbed down from the saddle. The gelding was steady but young, and the last place she wanted to be when a strange vehicle came blaring into the yard was atop an untried horse, especially as the driver of this particular vehicle seemed to have a heavy foot. Sure enough, by the time Neely had resettled her hat and walked across the training area, a dualie pickup truck with a horse trailer attached had topped the rise and shot straight past the house to come to a skidding halt in front of the barn.

Matt Ender came slamming out of the house, bareheaded and wearing a long, caped duster, bawling at the top of his lungs. "That's my horse you're hauling, Calcuddy! Have some care!"

"I know it's your horse," this Calcuddy shouted right back at him, bailing out of the truck cab. "You owe me seven hunnerd dollars for bringing him."

"Not if you've crippled him or skinned him, I don't," Matt argued.

They argued all the while they unloaded the animal, a big blue roan with black mane and tail. He was magnificent. She knew that Matt was a roper and a saddle bronc rider, so the roan had to be his roping horse. Neely didn't expect it to be a stud, but when the animal reared as soon as it cleared the loading ramp, she saw that it was. When she realized that they meant to turn it into the corral next to her barrel-racing setup, she immediately climbed up onto the common fence.

"Hey!" She waved her arm over her head. "No! Don't do that!"

Still bickering and fighting to control the whinnying horse, they didn't hear her. That or they ignored her. Hoping to catch the stud before it bolted, she climbed over the metal pipe fence and dropped down to the ground just as Matt opened the gate to the corral.

"Stop!" she shouted, but Calcuddy had already released the halter lead, and suddenly the roan was bearing down on her. She flapped her arms, trying to turn the stud, and heard Matt shout.

"Get out of the way!"

"It's open!" she shouted back. Then the stud was on her, rearing, its front hooves flashing high overhead.

An instant later something, someone, hit her from the side, knocking her to the ground, covering her completely. The stud galloped away.

"He's getting out!" She tried to push Matt off, even as she realized that he'd probably just saved her life.

"Are you crazy?" he yelled, sitting up and shaking her. "Challenging a stud horse that's been closed up in a trailer for hours on end is a good way to get killed."

"This corral is open to the pasture," she shouted back, "and there's another stud out there!"

Matt turned white beneath his tan and the scruff of his beard. "I didn't know that," he exclaimed, hopping to his feet. His bandaged hand went to the top of his head. Hissing, he pulled it down again, bringing it to his chest. She hoped he hadn't exacerbated the damage trying to help her, but there was no time to think of that now.

"The ATV," she said, pointing to the barn, even as she ran for the saddled horse in the starting chute.

He ran in the opposite direction, and a minute later, they were both riding across the open pasture. Matt had the halter lead in his teeth as he gunned the three-wheeler over the rutted ground. They caught up to the stud as it circled a trio of fillies with interest. Just then, Neely's bay, Blaze, came galloping over the hill to defend his harem, trumpeting a challenge. She took off after Blaze, driving him away, while Matt killed the engine on the ATV and talked his horse Blue into accepting a lead.

Thankfully, the big stud showed good training and allowed the lead to be clipped onto his halter. Once Matt started slowly homeward with Blue following docilely behind the ATV, Neely galloped her mount back to the barn. The gelding had behaved admirably and exhibited laudable speed; she had high hopes for him. After shucking the saddle, she started grooming the pale orange horse just before Matt and his stud arrived.

"So if you've ruined the corral, where am I supposed to put my horse?" he demanded, holding up his heavily bandaged hand like a club.

"I didn't ruin the corral," she shot back. "You just didn't close the back gate."

"I didn't know there *was* a back gate. It never had a back gate before."

"Well, it has a back gate *now*, Ender."

"Why?"

"Because I find it useful."

"You know, I don't really care what you find useful. This is *my* home, and the corral was never open to the pasture before."

"Things have changed," she told him smartly, tossing the curry brush into a bucket. "Get used to it."

"I don't have to get used to anything."

"Suit yourself." She started for the door at the front of the barn then suddenly whirled around. "Pick a stall, any stall, for your horse, but keep him away from my client's gelding. We can't afford to pay for an injured animal." With that she turned and stomped out of the building.

"We?" he called after her. "You and who else? You got a mouse in your pocket? There ain't no *we*, lady."

She hoped he was wrong. Matthew Ender had a claim on the ranch, so she needed him to be on board with the *we* she had put together with his grandmother. Her agreement with Sheryl was a verbal one; they'd signed no papers. It had seemed wiser to see how the arrangement worked out first. Then, when everything seemed to be working well, a more formal agreement hadn't seemed necessary. Now that he had come, suddenly everything she and Amber had here seemed at risk. Again.

Why did this keep happening to them?

Before their parents had died, they'd enjoyed an easy life of privilege. Neely had owned some of the fastest, most expensive barrel-racing horses in the world. Her folks had poured thousands into helping her get established as a barrel racer, and she'd come very close to a national title, thanks to them. She'd have had it, too, if she'd had just one more season.

Instead, she'd lost everything.

Neely tried to have faith that everything would work out, as Scripture promised, for their good, but sometimes it was difficult to see how that could be so.

All she could do was pray and work and pray and work. And pray.

The screen door slammed behind Matt as he stepped up into the kitchen. He gave the other door a good shove to make sure it followed, the glass in the window rattling as it banged shut. Outside, the sound of Calcuddy's rig spraying gravel as it tore out of the yard punctuated the ensuing silence.

"Something wrong?" Grandma asked mildly, sliding a fried chicken leg onto a plate for lunch.

"Do you know what that fool woman's done?" he demanded.

"Don't know any fool women around here," Sheryl retorted calmly.

He ignored that. "She's put a back gate in the corral, opened it to the pasture. I nearly lost my prize roping horse when some rogue stud came charging over the hill. If they'd fought, Blue could've been injured or killed. We got to him just in time."

"That 'rogue stud' is a highly prized barrel racer," Grandma Sheryl informed him, "and he's saved this ranch with his stud fees alone."

Dumbfounded, Matt stared as she finished dishing up the lunch. "Gran, why didn't you tell me the ranch was in trouble?"

She made a face, wrapped her hands in the skirt of her apron and twisted them anxiously. He realized again how tiny she was, shrunken to the size of a dried apple. "You and Marcus have your own lives," she finally said. "I didn't want to burden you with my troubles. But taxes don't pay themselves, you know, and eventually insurance money runs out."

He'd always known that his grandfather and father had left something but not how much. Apparently it hadn't been enough.

"Gran, I...I just assumed..."

"I couldn't keep the place up on my little bit of Social Security," she told him.

"I thought you got several thousand a month."

"Most of that went away when you boys did."

Matt felt about ten inches tall. He'd left home at eighteen, right after high school, eager to make his mark on the world. He'd never given a thought to how Gran was making it. She'd always seemed to be fine whenever he'd checked in.

"I didn't realize." But he should have.

"Neely has been the answer to a prayer, Matthew," Sheryl insisted. "That girl is a wonder with horses and gave up a promising career racing barrels to take care of her baby sister after their parents died."

He smacked himself in the forehead. Of course. *That* Neely Spencer. She'd come in second at the National Finals three years ago, then she'd just fallen off the face of the earth. He remembered her then, younger and thinner than she was now. She'd worn her hair with bangs back then. They'd grown down to her chin since, framing her pretty face while the rest of her hair fell to her shoulders.

Clearing his throat, he said, "Her parents died?"

"In an airplane crash. Newspaper reports said the pilot, her dad, was at fault somehow. Others were on board, business clients, I think. There were lawsuits. Between settlements and fines, those two girls lost everything, or very near it. I met Neely at a sale where I was letting go of the very last of my stock and she was about to put up her stud. We got to talking and one thing led to another, and here we are."

"I see," he said, and he did. He saw that he could have saved the ranch by doing just what Neely was doing, if only he hadn't been such a selfish no-account. He'd have known that the ranch needed saving in the first place if he hadn't basically abandoned his grandmother and the home place.

The throbbing in his hand reminded him that it had taken only a major injury to get him here now.

Chapter Two

The woman is too loving for her own good, Neely thought on Friday when Sheryl asked her to drive Matthew into town to see the doctor. The bounder had literally abandoned Sheryl, crawling home only when he had no place else to go, but she'd welcomed him back with open arms. Neely could spit fire over the whole thing, but seeing as how Sheryl had given her and Amber a home, helped her keep Blaze and put money in their pockets again, she kept her tongue firmly behind her teeth. She'd even agreed to help him by giving him a ride, although the only ride she *wanted* to give him was one straight out of town.

After all, she knew why Sheryl asked. He couldn't drive himself while chugging those pain meds, as he had done since he'd arrived in the middle of the night Wednesday, and Sheryl was basically housebound these days.

"When are you going to get your glasses replaced, Sheryl?" she asked.

"When I get my check," Sheryl answered, avoiding her gaze.

"You said that last month."

"This month for sure." Uh-huh. "Put five dollars on my layaway while you're in town?"

"Sure," Neely said. She was going to be paying on her own Christmas layaway, anyhow, and she could pick up Amber from school on her way home, save her the long bus ride. Just as Sheryl handed over the five dollars, Matthew came downstairs wearing a handsome pecan-brown wool cowboy hat with clean jeans and a polka-dot shirt.

"Ready to go, Gran?"

"Neely's driving you, hon." She dug another five-dollar bill out of her purse and waved it at Matt. "Pick up some of those chips and other snacks you like."

He kissed her on the cheek while gently pushing the money away, saying, "I'll take care of it."

Big of him to feed himself, Neely thought drily.

They gathered their coats and trekked outside. She went for the car; he headed for the truck. Both halted midway, speaking at the same time.

"You want to go in that?"

He chuckled. She grinned, in spite of herself.

"I need to pick up my sister on the way back," she said.

"No problem." He dug his keys out of the pocket of his jeans with his left hand and tossed them to her.

"Okay. I can drive that big, fancy truck."

"Easier than I can fold myself into that little car, I imagine," he said.

He had a point. Like most ropers, he was a big man, well over six feet tall and weighing maybe one-eighty. She climbed up into the truck, stowed her handbag and latched her seat belt then started up the engine and adjusted the seat position and mirrors. This was a sweet vehicle, power everything, state-of-the-art add-ons. She didn't even really need a key, just had to have the key fob in her possession to depress the starter.

"I could pull my trailer with this," she said, backing around with the help of the backup camera.

He looked behind them at the barn. "That's your trailer?"

"Yep. Couldn't keep the truck because it wasn't paid for, but there was no lien on the trailer, and a horse ranch needs one, so…"

"What were you planning to pull it with?" he asked, settling into his plush seat.

She aimed the truck down the drive. "I just need to train up one winner out of Blaze, then it won't be a problem. Until then, we'll have to keep begging and borrowing."

"So you're planning to breed and train barrel-racing horses?"

"Not planning," she said. "We're doing it. I'm taking other horses to train on the side to bring in extra money until our mares foal and the stock is old enough to train and sell."

"And you're also standing Blaze to stud."

"That's right. We funded the whole project that way."

"Not a bad business plan. You put the roof on the house that way?"

"Yeah, now that you mention it."

She glanced at him, saw that he sprawled there on the passenger's seat as if he were knocking back on the couch at the ranch. The pain meds must be working; he wasn't even holding his hand up.

"Truck's a dream," she said, smiling at his mellowness.

"I promised myself that if I ever made the finals, I'd buy one," he told her, "so that's what I did. First new one I've ever owned." He lifted off his hat with his left hand and rubbed the top of his head with his right, then hissed and dropped the injured hand to his lap.

She chuckled. "Your hair's a mess."

He flipped down the visor and opened the lighted mirror, smoothing the mess as best he could. "I had to cut it with my left hand this last time."

"You cut your own hair?"

"Not much time to find a barbershop when you're constantly rushing from one rodeo to another, and that's what it takes to make the finals."

"Yeah, I remember."

He closed the mirror and sat back, fitting his hat onto his head again. "Everybody thought you'd nail it that next year."

"Me included."

"Sorry about your folks," he said softly.

She nodded. "Thanks. Been tough on my little sister."

"Amber's a cute kid," he said. "I met her on the stairs last night as she was going up to bed." And he was going down to a late supper, having slept through the communal meal, the lazy bum. "She's kind of a mini version of you but with redder, curlier hair. How old is she? Eight? Nine?"

"Ten." Neely shifted in her seat, uncomfortable talking about her baby sis with him, and asked, "How did you hurt your hand?"

When he explained, she had to rethink her silent criticism. No wonder he was popping pain pills. "Whoa. Tore off all the flesh?"

"Thankfully it was all there inside the glove," he said, "so they were able to reattach everything. I hope. I can't move it yet, so I don't know that it actually bends, but the tissue is alive. Or it was when I left Florida. And they tell me that's half the battle."

"What happens if it doesn't bend?"

"Then I'll have no grip," he told her shortly.

No grip on his right hand. His career would be over. It might well be anyway.

"I'll pray for you," she said, gripping the steering wheel with both hands.

"Been praying since it happened."

That rocked her back somewhat. A praying Matt Ender didn't fit her image of a man who was only concerned about himself.

She parked the truck at the doctor's office twenty minutes later, told Matt she had business at the mercantile and strode off, huddled inside her sheepskin-lined jean jacket. She pulled a striped knit cap from her pocket and pulled it on to keep her ears warm as she walked. She expected to complete her errand and return to either wait in the truck or find him waiting. She stood in line at the layaway counter for nine or ten minutes, made both payments and then got sidetracked by a new display of striped leggings. The sound of Matt's voice some minutes later caught her completely off guard.

"You'd look cute in those."

She jumped, suddenly aware that she'd been humming along to the Christmas music in the background. "They're for Amber."

"Oh. Well, she'll look cute in them, too."

"You weren't at the doctor's long."

He held up his hand, showing off a fresh bandage.

"Nope. He unwrapped it, confirmed that the flesh is pink and doesn't stink, squirted all the incisions with antibiotic and antiseptic and wrapped it up again." He lowered the hand, adding, "No movement yet."

"It's probably too early," she said, hoping that was true, for both their sakes. If Matt couldn't rope, he couldn't compete, and if he couldn't compete, he might decide to stay at the ranch, in which case, she might well find herself looking for some place else to go.

But there was no sense in worrying about it now. She picked up two pairs of the leggings. They were cheap, and they'd give Amber something to look forward to; a wrapped Christmas package around the house was always fun.

He glanced about, asking, "What would you suggest I get Grandma Sheryl for Christmas? I mean, what does she need most?"

"Glasses." He seemed surprised, looking toward housewares. "Not drinking glasses, eyeglasses. She broke hers weeks ago and can't afford to replace them. They were so old she'll no doubt need a new exam. That's why she didn't drive you into town today. She can't see well enough to drive."

"That can't wait for Christmas," he said, frowning. Then he reached into his coat and plucked a receipt from a pocket, asking, "Why did she owe the doctor two hundred and thirty-seven bucks?"

"You paid her doctor bill?"

He nodded. "They took my money, but they wouldn't tell me why she owed it."

"It's nothing serious, a little low blood pressure, some tests. I imagine the bill has been accumulating over time and they've let it ride."

He stuffed the paper back into his pocket. "What about that Christmas gift?"

She stood staring at him for several seconds. "She could really use a good pair of boots."

Matt grinned. "Let's throw around a little cash."

She rolled her eyes. Easy come, easy go, just like every rodeo playboy she'd ever known, but she was more than willing to let him spend his money on Sheryl.

They chose a pair of distressed black goat leather in-laid with turquoise. Matt actually wanted something a little flashier, but they didn't have them small enough to fit Sheryl.

"We need a tree," he said as soon as they hit the street with their wrapped packages. "Don't you think?"

She had promised Amber a Christmas tree as soon as the Wheatons paid her for training the gelding. Claire's twelfth birthday fell on the nineteenth of December, and Noble wanted the horse ready for his daughter by then, but that was two weeks away yet. Neely checked her watch.

"We don't have much time if we're going to get to the school before the buses leave."

"Better hurry then."

They rushed, and it was worth it when they pulled up next to the school and Neely tooted the horn on the truck then rolled down the window to wave at Amber, who was standing in line for the bus. Her bright red head jerked around, curls bouncing. She recognized the truck, saw Neely behind the wheel and spied the spruce in the bed.

"We got a tree!" she squealed, breaking ranks and running for the vehicle.

Neely waved to the teacher on bus duty as Amber

piled into the backseat of the cab, backpack and lunch bag in tow.

"Hi, Matt."

He doffed his hat with his left hand. "Miss Amber."

"Nice hat." She giggled and Neely fought the urge to be annoyed. What was Amber doing making friends with the man? Didn't she realize what a threat he was to their situation? If his competing days were over, he could very well be planning to take over the ranch and put her and her sister out on the street. Again. But not without a fight. She and Sheryl might not have a formal contract, but they did have a well-known agreement. He might as well understand up front that she wouldn't go easily.

Neely prayed silently as she drove, asking for clarity of thought and speech. When they got to the house, she told Amber to go inside and help Sheryl make a place for the tree. Then she caught Matt's arm before he could get out of the truck.

"I think it's time for a little plain speaking."

He smiled, but his dark eyes narrowed beneath the brim of his hat. "About?"

"My partnership with your grandmother."

"Ah," he said, nodding. "Well, Gran told me you met at a horse sale."

"That's right. She was selling the last of her stock, a couple of broke-down old mares. I'd come to the conclusion that I couldn't afford to hang on to my horses anymore. Dixie had already sold, and I was trying to work myself up to parting with Blaze when Sheryl put an arm around my shoulders and offered to pray for me. Turned out she was my answer to that prayer. She had the land I couldn't afford. I had Blaze and some capital after selling Dixie. We decided to join forces."

"How's that been going?" he asked.

She cocked her head. "We're not getting rich yet, but we've settled the back taxes, made some repairs and are paying the bills. We've been able to buy some decent brood stock. Sheryl's even planning on branching out. She's got your brother picking up some stock for her in Colorado now, I believe. She's been kind of hush-hush about that."

He nodded. "I know Marcus is glad to help. If I'd known she needed anything, I'd have sent her money, and I know that Marcus would've, too, but she never said a word, not to me, and I doubt she said much of anything to him, either." He reached across with his left hand and covered hers, where it lay on the center console. "Thank you for helping her." With that, he got out of the truck and trudged around to the bed to let down the tailgate.

Well, that hadn't gone exactly as she'd planned, but at least he had a thorough understanding of the situation. She got out and went to help him with the tree. Grasping the trunk with his one good hand, he pulled the seven-foot spruce forward. Neely hurried to seize the narrow end of the tree and help him carry it into the house. By the time they got it there, she realized that he was in serious pain. Nevertheless, he helped get the tree into the stand before he collapsed into a chair.

For the first time, Neely didn't mind when Sheryl hurried to coddle him with pills, a warm cup of apple cider and a crocheted afghan thrown around his shoulders. He was asleep on the couch long before they'd finished decorating the tree.

* * *

Being coddled was a welcome luxury for Matt. Women had been few and far between in his life, especially good women. His mother had run out on the family just after his ninth birthday. He still remembered all too vividly her alcohol-fueled crying jags and how his dad had pleaded with her to give up the drinking. She'd left with some guy who enjoyed the booze as much as she did. That's when his dad had moved him and his brother back to the ranch to live.

Grandma Sheryl had always been a no-nonsense type, but loving in her calm, pragmatic way. Still, Matt knew he hadn't really let her get too close. The sting of his mother's abandonment had left him hurting and gun-shy. After his dad had died, killed in a tractor incident while sowing a hayfield more than half a mile from the house when Matt was thirteen, Matt had turned into quite a handful. He'd never told anyone, but Matt couldn't help feeling that he should've been there for his father that day instead of off with his friends. Gran had tried to coddle him then, but he'd been too angry to accept her loving, and they'd butted heads more often than not, for all the good it had done either of them. He wished he'd had the sense to let her coddle him a little back then. Things might have been different if he had. They might have finally built the relationship they should have had all along—one where she felt comfortable turning to him for help when she needed it.

He mulled that over as he admired the colored lights on the Christmas tree in the corner and stretched the kinks out of his back after spending the night stretched out on the couch. He wondered who had removed his boots, then his stomach growled and he realized he had missed dinner. Just as he jackknifed into a sitting position, Amber's head popped up over the back of the couch.

"He's up!" she bawled, shouting right into his ear. His eyes crossed as his startled movement caused pain to blossom in his hand.

"Morning to you, too," he muttered, cutting her a glance as she skirted the end of the threadbare couch and plopped down on it.

He reached for the pill bottle, popped the top with his good thumb and dug out two capsules with his index finger. After pausing to take stock, however, he decided on one pill for now and swallowed that.

Amber picked up the remote control from the end table and pointed it at the TV, saying, "I thought you were gonna sleep through my show."

"Sorry."

"Oh, and Sheryl said to tell you breakfast is ready when you are."

"In that case…" He reached for his boots, shoved his feet down inside them and stood.

When he got to the kitchen a minute later, he didn't find Sheryl at the stove but Neely. She pulled a plate of biscuits from the oven and carried them to the table then brought over a skillet of gravy.

"Thanks. Coffee?" he asked.

"Fresh pot."

She pulled the basket from the stovetop percolator and emptied it into the can that Gran kept for that purpose. He got a mug down from the cabinet, filled it and set it on the scarred top of the old round table. Neely got out a plate and fork for him. Then she walked over to the rolltop desk in the corner and pulled a small laptop from a cubby. After powering it up, she took a pen and jotted something down on a bit of paper before carrying the paper to the table and slapping it down next to his plate.

"Sheryl thought you might feel well enough today to go over the books with her after you eat."

"The books?"

"Financial records. That's my password and that's the file. She's not much with the computer, but I figure you can handle it."

He had said something to Gran that first day about checking the books. Tucking the paper into his shirt pocket, he squinted a smile up at her. "Thanks."

"No problem. I'll go take care of the horses." With that, she left the room.

Matt shrugged and dug into the biscuits and gravy. It couldn't hurt to be sure everything was organized. Man, he'd forgotten how good Gran's biscuits and gravy were, not to mention coffee percolated on a stovetop over an open flame. He could get used to eating like this again. And to seeing a pretty woman around the table every morning.

Gran came in before he finished his second helping, carrying a stack of ledgers.

"Neely's got her ways, and I've got mine," she announced. "She thinks you'll want to compare both sets of books, but I told her that wouldn't be necessary."

He waved his bandaged hand in a stalling gesture. "Doesn't hurt to be thorough."

Sheryl dropped the books onto the desk. "Matthew Eric Ender. How can you not trust Neely?"

He spread his hands. "I didn't say I don't trust her.

I just think if you're going to do something, you ought to do it right. Right?"

Narrowing her eyes at him, Sheryl slapped open the first book. Matt got up and moved to the desk. Sheryl turned a dining chair and sat down next to him. He took the paper from his pocket and pecked in the password then searched through Neely's files until he found the right one. With Sheryl at his side, they went over the figures in the various columns and ledgers. Everything added up to the penny, and he couldn't help being impressed with what Neely and Gran had accomplished thus far. It irked him that Gran had to almost put her nose to the page to read her own writing, however.

"Come Monday morning, we're going into town and getting you new eyeglasses," he said.

She sat back, huffing her irritation. He'd heard that sound more times than he could count. It made him grin because this time he hadn't done anything wrong.

"I'm going to heat up some coffee," she announced, nose in the air.

While she did that, he poked around in some of Neely's other files. He found her Christmas lists for Amber and Gran, her training schedule, which he had to approve of, and her to-do list, which surprised him with its pragmatic approach and accurate cost estimates. When he stumbled across an instant messaging conversation with someone named Noble, he couldn't help scanning it. Finding that Neely had an admirer came as no surprise, but it soured his stomach, nonetheless, especially as the guy laid it on thick with comments such as "Can't stop thinking about you" and "Your beauty always stuns me." Neely didn't appear to be buying it. Her replies consisted of polite thanks and "Stop. You're making me blush." Noble remarked that he couldn't wait until he could ask her out, so apparently they were still dancing around each other.

Matt found himself wondering if he could cut in, but then he shook his head. What would be the point in that? He wasn't planning to stay around longer than he had to in order to mend and get back into shape. Even though Neely interested him. Okay, she more than interested him. What she'd pulled off here was nothing short of genius—as a horse trainer himself, he should know—and the woman got prettier every time he saw her. But his life was with the rodeo. He hoped.

Gran carried two mugs back to the desk and he quickly closed out the file, leaving up the financial one. They went back to the figures, though he was just going through the motions now. Neely had done good work here. Gran was blessed to have her, and he intended to tell Neely so.

A vehicle pulled into the yard, and he turned at the same time Gran did to look out the kitchen window. The late-model luxury sedan that parked next to Gran's battered little compact had Matt craning his neck.

"Who's that?"

Gran made a dismissive gesture. "Oh, that's Neely's client, the owner of the butternut gelding she's training."

Matt searched his mind for the name, lifting his hand to the top of his head. "Uh, Wheaton?"

"Mmm-hmm. Noble Wheaton. Neely's training the horse for his daughter."

Noble. Aha. Wait. "Daughter! The guy's married?" If so, that would explain why he couldn't ask Neely out. But then why would he expect to be able to ask her out soon? Was he going through a divorce?

"Widowed," Gran said.

Matt was out of his chair before he even realized he was going to move.

"What on earth?" Sheryl asked.

He looked down at her, momentarily stymied, but then his brain kicked in and he put on a smile. "I think I need some air."

She rolled her eyes. "Sleeping on the couch has crimped your spine and cut off oxygen to your brain."

"There you go," he agreed, striding through the house in search of his hat and duster.

It occurred to him as he shrugged into the coat that when Marcus showed up, one of them would have to sleep on the couch or they'd be sharing a room. Maybe he should build onto the house. Two more rooms would do it, a bedroom and a bathroom. Sharing a bathroom with three women was turning out to be something of a trial.

He turned that thought off, and then he told himself that building on was a bad idea. Neither he nor Marcus was apt to be around enough to make it cost-effective. Unless his hand didn't heal properly.

What then? Matt shoved that concern to the back of his mind and left the house by the front door, walking around the porch to the side steps by the kitchen. He'd look in on Blue and take the measure of this Noble Wheaton who drove a luxury car and wrote love letters to Neely Spence. And then?

Matt honestly had no idea.

Chapter Three

"I think you'll see that he's coming along just fine," Neely said, leading the saddled bay from the barn. Frisky on this crisp Saturday morning, the horse danced sideways around Noble, who stood dead center of the yard, as solid and square as a brick column in his slacks and expensive leather coat. The hat that perched atop his prematurely graying buzz haircut could have paid for Amber's entire Christmas.

To Neely's consternation, Matthew stepped off the porch and walked around both cars. Tall and lean, he wore the caped duster and broad-brimmed hat as if born to them. Beside him, Noble Wheaton looked slightly... ridiculous. Wealthy but ridiculous, as if he didn't quite belong. It irked Neely that Matt could so easily show up Noble for what he was—too old, pudgy and about as much cowboy as that New York nanny on Amber's favorite TV show. And here Neely had been trying to convince herself that Noble Wheaton was all a girl could ever want.

If she was honest with herself, she had refrained from encouraging Noble's romantic intentions for some time now, though he'd made his interest in her more than obvious. Oh, all right. He'd been downright cloying about it, instant messaging her, sending notes with his payments, buying her silly little gifts, most of which were utterly useless. She even had to make sure that Amber and Sheryl sat on each side of her in church to keep him from encroaching there. He still managed to stay close because his daughter and Amber were friends. Though Claire was a grade ahead of Amber, the two girls liked to sit together.

Noble eyed Matthew with a frown and a discernible twitch of his nose. "Don't I know you?"

"Maybe. Been around these parts long?"

"My whole life."

"Well, then, you just might remember me," Matt said, keeping his hands behind his back. "Matthew Ender."

Noble's heavy features looked like chiseled stone all of a sudden. "You were the troublemaker."

Matt grinned. "That would be me. About, oh, fourteen, fifteen years ago. Can't say as I remember you, though. Must have passed through high school before my time."

At least six or seven years before Matt's time, Neely guessed. She said, "Matt, you don't have a stopwatch, do you? I was just about to show Mr. Wheaton what Buttercup here can do."

"Buttercup!" Matt laughed, gesturing with his good hand toward the horse. "Who named this handsome animal *Buttercup*?"

Beside him, Noble did a slow burn, muttering, "My daughter picked that name. To her, a horse is a horse. She's too young to think about gender and such things. It's her horse. She can name him what she likes."

Matt looked at Neely, leaned forward slightly and said, sotto voice, "Remind me to give Amber lessons in horse naming."

She did her best not to roll her eyes. Or laugh. Amber, after all, had campaigned for a number of other names, anything but Buttercup, for the powerful gelding.

In her most businesslike tone, she asked, "Do you happen to have a stopwatch or not?"

"On my phone," he said, pulling the thing from his pocket.

"Would you position yourself by the barrier, please?"

"Glad to help."

Glad to make trouble, she thought as he trotted off to open the gate and take up his post. *Not so much has changed in the past decade and a half, after all.*

She led the horse through the gate and across the plowed training ground, then mounted up and took a few gallops around the fence line before riding the gelding into the long, wide starting chute. Backing him to the very end, she felt him dancing beneath her. In another week, she'd take down the back fence on this chute and let him have the feel of the open alley, but not today. The instant he began to quiet beneath her, she flapped both legs, and he took off like a rocket. The barrier string zinged as they burst past it, and she hoped Matt had a quick left thumb.

Thinking about that reminded her to bear left. The horse cut around the barrel, leaning hard, then straightened and raced, long legs stretching full out, to the opposite barrel. Again, they swung tightly left, all the way around. Then he was eating up the ground with his long, even strides to the far barrel at the apex of the triangle. One more deep, left-leaning circle, this one a little wider than she'd have liked, and they were flying for home, the horse's legs stretching, hers flapping.

Matt was up on the fence before she got the bay reined in. "Why the left turns? You didn't run left when you were racing before."

Ignoring the pleasant thought that he'd remembered or researched her past runs, she turned the horse and let him trot back Matt's way. "Claire Wheaton is left-handed."

"Left-handed and inexperienced, I take it."

"Exactly."

Grinning, he showed her the time as she passed. She rode right up to Noble. "That's almost five seconds off the last timed run. Of course, that's with an experienced hand riding. Claire will have to be taught to handle him herself."

Noble smiled up at her. "I'm sure you can teach her everything she needs to know. The horse will be ready by her birthday, yes?"

"He's ready now," she said. "Good barrel horses always need work, though. You can't just let them sit. You have to constantly reinforce the training."

"I understand," he told her. "I just want to make sure that when I put my Claire up in the saddle, the horse beneath her is as well trained as it can be."

"I give you my word on that."

"Excellent. Let me help you down," he said, reaching for her.

She swung off by herself, saying lightly, "No need. I'm used to mounting and dismounting on my own."

"I would help you with a great many things if you'd let me," he told her softly.

Matt arrived just then, saying, "That's what a real

professional job looks like. You know, Wheaton, lots of trainers train their way and expect the rider to adapt. Neely is doing you a real favor by training this horse to work with a left-handed racer."

Noble smiled, if such a cold thing could be called a smile. "I'm from the school that believes a man should get what he pays for."

"And I'm from the school that believes a man should know when to be grateful," Matt returned smoothly. He looked at Neely then and tipped his hat.

Noble grasped Neely by the shoulders as if to capture her attention and turn her away from Matthew entirely. "Neely knows how I feel about her," he said. Then, "I'll see you in church tomorrow, my dear."

She just nodded and when the horse shifted, she used that as an excuse to step back out of his grasp, her hands tightening on the reins.

Noble turned a sour expression on Matt, saying, "Since we're not likely to see each other again, I'll say goodbye, sir."

"Oh, no," Matt said, his hands again tucked behind his back. "I'll be around for quite some time. I'm sure we'll bump into each other again. Like tomorrow, for instance. At church. Wouldn't miss it."

Noble couldn't very well complain about that, though his expression looked anything but pleasant, despite his words. "Well, that's fine. That's just…fine."

Matt grinned and stood there until Noble got into his car and left. Neely let out a breath she hadn't realized she'd been holding and shot Matt Ender a scolding glance. "You haven't changed much in the last fifteen years, have you?"

"I don't know about that, *my dear*," he said, drop-

ping his voice into husky territory on the last two words.
She rolled her eyes. Laughing, he asked, "Need any
more help?"

"No, thanks."

"Good. My hand hurts like the very dickens."

"I'm sure it does."

She led the bay toward the corral, thinking to give
the horse a good canter while she had him saddled.

"Neely," Matt called.

"Yeah?"

"Good work."

She wished that didn't make her smile. She wished
so much about him didn't make her smile. Why couldn't
Noble make her smile?

Some questions, it seemed, just had no answers.

Grandma Sheryl's surprise couldn't have been more
obvious when Matt came downstairs on Sunday morning in his best jeans and a white shirt and black string
tie worn beneath a camel tan corduroy sport coat. Neely
looked alternately pleased then irritated by his outfit.
He had the feeling she was weighing how Noble Wheaton would react to his polished-up appearance. Only
Amber, her bright red curls blazing in the early morning sun pouring through the kitchen window, seemed
to take his upgrade in looks in stride.

"Ain't you gonna shave for church?"

He palmed the scruff on his jaw and chin. "This
is shaved, curly. I work to keep my whiskers just this
length."

"*Ain't* isn't a word," Neely corrected softly.

Amber ignored her, asking Matt, "Don't they scratch?"

"You tell me," he teased, engulfing her with his good

left arm and rubbing his cheek against hers while she giggled and squirmed in her chair at the table.

"They're soft!" she announced in surprise when he backed off.

"Uh-huh. I work at keeping them that way. If I shave every day, my beard's constantly prickly. This way they're soft. Besides, don't you think I'm cute with whiskers?" He batted his eyelashes at her.

She cut her sister a conspiratorial glance. "Neely does."

He fought the urge to look at Neely and gauge her reaction to that. "'Course she does. Grandma Sheryl does, too. Don't you, Gran?" He moved to the stove, where Gran was scrambling an egg.

"I think you're going to make us late to church if you don't eat right now."

"Got a travel mug for the coffee?" he asked, reaching for two slices of bread. "I'll make a sandwich of this and eat it on the way."

Neely set a stainless steel travel mug on the counter next to the range, muttering, "Maybe you ought to start getting ready a little earlier next time."

"That'd be great advice," he said, "if there weren't three women and one bathroom in this house."

"I'll get my Bible," Gran told no one in particular and walked away. Neely followed.

Finished building the sandwich with slices of bacon and scrambled egg, Matt carried it to the table, where he wrapped it in a paper napkin.

"Neely does think you're cute," Amber whispered, "but she don't trust you."

Matt tried not to let the sting of that show. "No? How come?"

"She thinks you'll put us out on our ears."

That surprised him. He had nothing but admiration for what Neely had done here. "I won't do that," he said.

"What will you do?" the girl asked, all big blue eyes and flaming red curls. Surprised that he really didn't know what he was going to do about anything, he winked.

"I'll go to church."

That's exactly what he did, what they all did. At his insistence, they piled into his truck, with Neely driving, and headed off. Grandma Sheryl and Amber had decorated the porch for Christmas on Saturday, twining the railing with ivy and cedar boughs fastened in place with big red bows. As he munched his breakfast sandwich and guzzled coffee from the travel mug, Matt thought that the greenery made a pretty display. Having these Spence girls around made all the difference when it came to Christmas. He just wished Neely would stop treating him like the villain of the piece. As they made the drive to church, he determined to behave more cordially.

So far as he could tell from the graveled parking lot, nothing much had changed at the Red Bluff Countryside Church since his childhood, save for the sign identifying it. Situated a mile or so outside town on a flat, treeless field, the concrete block building had been painted white so many times that the indentations between the blocks barely showed. It still offered a drive-through shelter from the elements and a double glass door entry, as well as a huge cross made of steel girders, flanked by the Oklahoma state and US flags.

"Where'd the sign come from?"

A big, flashy neon thing atop two poles that replicated the steel cross and announced the name of the church in big block letters, it seemed rather out of place.

"Claire's daddy did that," Amber supplied from the backseat.

Claire's daddy. Hadn't he heard Claire's name just the other day? "That would be... Noble Wheaton?" Matt guessed.

"Noble's been very generous with the church," Sheryl said. Neely said nothing.

"I bet he has," Matt murmured.

Neely shot him an unreadable glance and turned the truck into an empty space.

"Leave your hat in the truck, Matt," Grandma said. "There're never enough hooks for all the hats."

"Yes, ma'am," he said, ducking his head and lifting it off. Doors opened and cold winter wind whipped into the vehicle. He left the hat on the center console, saying to Neely, "Someone ought to get Noble Wheaton to donate more hat hooks."

She said nothing, just tossed the keys into his lap and slid out on her side. He rubbed the top of his head, chuckling, and let himself out into the cold. Quickly catching up with her, he walked by her side toward the building, Gran and Amber having already disappeared.

"Want to tell me why you're doing this?" she asked suddenly.

"Going to church?" he clarified. "Believe it or not, church is usually where I go on Sunday."

"I'm sure."

"You never attended Cowboy Church while you were competing?"

He'd found the services held at rodeo contests throughout the country to be a comfort and a help.

They'd become so popular that they'd even spun off a permanent church movement with stationary buildings and memberships. Because so many rodeos were held over weekends, Sundays included, the Cowboy Church services were often the only ones that contestants got to attend. Since he'd started attending regularly, things had turned around for him, until recently, anyway.

Inside the Red Bluff church, quite a few folks recognized Matt and, upon seeing his bandaged hand, offered to pray for him. He welcomed their prayers.

"I'll take all the prayer I can get," he told them, smiling.

The place had been decorated to the rafters for Christmas, with greenery, lights, big red bows and poinsettias everywhere. He felt surrounded by Christmas, with Gran on one side and Neely on the other and the air filled with the scent of pine along with the sound of carols softly playing in the background. Amber sat between her sister and her friend Claire, a delicate child with long straight hair the same color as her horse and a frilly dress. Noble Wheaton took the other place next to his daughter, his possessive gaze traveling between her and Neely. Matt noticed that Wheaton hadn't left his hat in the car or hung it on a hook. Instead, he placed it on the pew next to him, as if it deserved as much space as old Mrs. Grady, Matt's third-grade teacher, who sat beside it.

Matt looked at the printed bulletin in his hand. "Huh, look at that, one of my favorite praise songs."

Sheryl peered at the printed page, where his left thumb pointed. "You know that song?"

"Never thought of it as a Christmas song, though,"

he said, beginning to softly sing the words. After a moment he looked up in surprise. "Guess it is, at that."

"I suppose a lot of the songs we sing in church could be thought of as Christmas songs, though we don't sing them just at Christmastime," Neely commented.

"Hadn't considered it," Matt admitted. "I suppose you're right."

She looked away, a slight crease between her brows, as if she didn't like it when he agreed with her.

Matt thoroughly enjoyed the service. One thing had changed. The current pastor was quite a bit younger and more dynamic than the last one. In fact, he couldn't have been more than five years Matt's senior. That fact made Matt feel a bit…immature. He couldn't help wondering where he'd be five years from now. Settled with a family of his own or still running from rodeo to rodeo trying to make a name for himself? The thought made him uncomfortable. He reached up with his hand, realized that rubbing his head in church might look odd and dropped the hand to his lap again.

After the service, Gran stepped across the aisle to speak to a friend. Wheaton, meanwhile, squeezed past the girls, hat in hand, to address Neely directly.

"Claire and I would love it if you and Amber would join us for lunch today."

Neely blinked, clearly caught off guard, and put on a regretful smile. "I'm sorry, but I have to drive the others home." Listening unabashedly, Matt lifted his injured right hand to lend credence to her excuse. "And, um, Sheryl has put on a pot roast," Neely added. "It's Matt's first Sunday back home."

"Aw, Neely," Amber wheedled.

"My first Sunday home," Matt told her, holding up

his bad hand and thumping himself in the chest with his good one. "You're not going to disappoint me, now, are you, curly?"

Amber sighed. Claire folded her arms, glaring at her father mulishly.

"Perhaps some other time," Neely said to the girls.

"We better let you get on, then," Wheaton rumbled, turning his daughter with one heavy hand.

Matt beamed at him. "Don't want that roast to overcook."

Amber followed Wheaton and his daughter along the pew and out into the aisle on the other end, chattering to Claire. Neely sent Matt an exasperated look, her blue eyes widening, and made as if to slip past him into the aisle behind Sheryl. He stepped into her way.

"What?" he questioned.

She shook her head. "Nothing."

"Let me ask you something," he said, keeping his voice low. "Are you and old Noble dating?"

She winced at the "old Noble," but then she shook her head, her gaze kept carefully averted. "We are not."

"Oh. 'Cause he sure seems to think he's got a claim on you."

Her blue gaze zipped up to meet his. "For your information, that's the first time he's ever invited my sister and me anywhere."

"Ah." In other words, Matt's presence had forced Wheaton's hand. Interesting.

"Now let me ask *you* something," she said. "When are you going to be able to rope and ride competitively again?"

"I don't know," he answered honestly. "Maybe never." It all depended on the strength of his grip once his hand healed. If he couldn't control a loop, couldn't grasp that hack rein, then he couldn't be either a roper or a saddle bronc rider anymore. He was too tall for bull riding, too slender for steer wrestling, too old to go to bare-back now, even if his hand should prove stable enough for the rigging. Besides, a single event wouldn't get him into the finals or provide a decent living.

She looked as if she might cry, and as much as he'd have liked to believe it, he didn't think her dismay was for his injury. "Does that mean you'd be staying at the ranch permanently then?"

"Maybe so," he told her, "but—"

He didn't get the chance to say more, as she abruptly shouldered past him, saying, "Excuse me, please."

Watching her take off up the aisle, he wished he'd handled that differently. He knew what was bothering her, after all. She was afraid he was going to upset her apple cart. Well, she was upsetting his. Coming home again to stay, if that's what he had to do, would be a far sight more difficult with the tempting Miss Neely Spence on the premises, unless… He lifted his hand to the top of his head, not liking where his thoughts were going, not liking it one little bit.

If Matthew stayed on the ranch, Neely told herself, then she and Amber would have to go. The house wasn't big enough for all of them. The business wasn't big enough for all of them. She just didn't see any way to make it work with him in the picture. Maybe he'd get a job in town, but she doubted he'd want to look for an apartment or house instead of staying with Sheryl. No, he'd expect her and Amber to move out to make room for him, but she didn't have enough money for that and wouldn't have for some time to come.

As she worked Buttercup on Monday morning, she wished that she hadn't spent half of what Noble had already paid her on Christmas presents, but how could she not? Amber had known lavish Christmases until three years ago. Then suddenly, at the age of seven, Amber's world had fallen apart. That first Christmas after the deaths of their parents had been terrible. Amber had sobbed most of the day, and they'd had only the kindness of friends to sustain them. The next year had been little better. But this year…this year it had begun to feel as if they'd turned a corner, as if they had a home again and all would be well. Until Matthew Ender had come.

It wasn't his fault that he had been injured, of course, but Neely couldn't help resenting his presence in her carefully ordered but terribly precarious world. She wondered if God was telling her that she should be encouraging Noble Wheaton, after all.

Before she could carry that thought any further, Matt came out of the house, ambling across the dusty yard in his hat and long coat. Why did he have to be so good-looking anyway? "Cute," Amber kept saying, but cute didn't begin to cover it. Matt was all man, all cowboy, all gorgeous. Neely wished she'd never laid eyes on him.

He climbed up on the fence and watched her put Buttercup through his paces then hopped down as she walked the horse to cool him off.

"That was some workout," he said. "Pity you can't do more."

She tried not to react to that but couldn't help herself. "How so?"

"Well, if you were a man," he said, "you could give my Blue a workout. I'm sure he's needing it by now."

Stopping in her tracks, she glared at him around Buttercup's nose. "I'll have you know that I can throw a loop as well as any man. If I were big enough to throw a calf, too, I could've given you a run for your money."

He grinned and drawled, "Is that so? Well, there's an old mechanical roping dummy in the barn. If it still works, I'll saddle the stud and you can show me just how talented you are."

What could she do but agree?

Chapter Four

The rubber calf's body fit over a bale of hay, which in turn sat on a spike attached to a chain that lurched at various speeds between two drive wheels spaced about forty feet apart in the roping arena. As roping machines went, this one was pretty low-tech and basic, a very early model, but Neely helped Matt cart it out to the corral and set it up. Operated by a small, gas-powered engine, the thing looked rusted and broken down, but to her surprise, he had it working again inside of half an hour. Armed with an oil can and a steel brush, he kept it going for several trial runs, the rubber calf's head bouncing along challengingly as the chain moved from the starting point to the end and then rewound.

Using temporary fencing rails, they set up a box, the starting point for the horse and roper, and strung a barrier across it, using the automatic release from Neely's barrel-racing setup. It was very important that the horse practice not breaking that barrier. The calf had to get a clean release before the roper could go after it. Breaking the barrier added penalty seconds to his time.

"You don't need a pigging string because there are

no legs to tie," Matt instructed her, hauling his saddle over to Blue's stall with his good hand. "But you do have to reach down and move three levers under the hay bale. That tips the bale to the side. When that happens, throw up your arms and get back in the saddle. Blue will take over from there."

As they saddled him, the stud proved fractious from his days of inactivity. Matt wound up at his head, calming him, while Neely took care of the girth. Then Matt walked the big roan out into the corral, tossed Neely up into the saddle and adjusted the slanting stirrups for her. Blue was a big one, easily nineteen hands tall. Buttercup, conversely, stood on the small side, about fifteen and a half hands. The ground looked a long way down from Blue's back. The stirrups slanted to make dismounting easier and quicker.

"Give him a trot while I find a rope."

She did that, letting Blue dance around and around the arena, moving him closer and closer to the roping dummy until he got a good sniff of it. He didn't like the thing one bit and showed it by kicking up his rear hooves. She stayed firm in the saddle, a bit white knuckled with her grip on the saddle horn, but calm. It never paid to let a horse know you were afraid. Matt returned with a pair of gloves and a thirty-foot poly-grass rope with a red eye and leather burner.

"Don't get caught in the dally," he warned, holding up his bandaged right hand, "not that you'll get a lot of resistance from this thing." He nodded toward the dummy and handed over the gear.

The instant she dropped the coiled rope around the saddle horn so she could pull on the gloves, the horse changed. A shiver went through him, and he was suddenly all business. He started looking for the box immediately, backing and swinging his big head around.

"He's ready to load," Matt said proudly, backing away. "Back him into the corner. He likes the left side, your left. Let me set up."

She maneuvered the stud into the left side corner, feeling him quiver beneath her. Shaking out the loop, she gave it a few practice twirls. Blue clamped the bit between his teeth and cocked a back hoof. Matt set the barrier and jogged over to start the motor on the roping machine then hurriedly returned her way.

"That's a lot of loop."

"Who's doing this?" she called. "You or me?"

"Your show," he said. Suddenly the dummy lunged forward. Matt released the barrier.

Before she could even touch her heels to the roan's sides, he was out of there. They nearly overran the dummy. She dropped the loop, dallied the rope around the saddle horn, being sure to keep her glove well out of the loop, and bailed off the stud. The corral hadn't been plowed in some time, so the impact jarred her teeth, but she ran for the dummy and searched frantically for the levers. She finally found them all, and the hay bale flopped over, killing the engine on the thing.

"Hands! Hands!" Matt yelled. She threw up her hands, and the horse backed away, keeping the rope taut as she raced back to haul herself up into the saddle. In a real-life situation, that would be very important. A live calf would struggle and try to release its legs. Should it get free from the pigging string tied around three of its legs within the first six seconds after the roper caught and tied it, then the roper would be disqualified. Keeping the rope taut reduced the likelihood of the calf getting free.

Matt came running out to her, chortling. "Not bad. You wouldn't win any money on that throw, but Blue's happy."

She looked down at the horse, still leaning against the rope to hold it taut. Something told her Blue would stand there all day keeping that rope tightly drawn until somebody released him.

"Ease up," Matt ordered, and the horse instantly relaxed. "Coil your rope," he told Neely. "I'll set up again."

This time, she kept her loop smaller, realizing that Blue had backpedaled before to help draw that loop tight as quickly as possible. She'd made more work for him with her big loop. Matt sped up the machine, too, and things went more smoothly, like clockwork, in fact. Neely began to think she couldn't miss, not with the machine, anyway. For argument's sake, she tried to aim Blue off course. He didn't go for it. The horse did exactly what he was trained to do, every time. He even obeyed her voice command to ease up. Seeing what she was up to, Matt moved the machine, canting it so the dummy ran at an angle. Blue adjusted beautifully. The big stud seemed to relish the challenge, in fact. Finally, his sides heaving, Neely walked the horse to cool him off then took him into the barn for a rubdown.

"That is one well-trained animal," she told Matt, who grinned.

"Yep. In my opinion, Blue's the best there's ever been."

"Who trained him?" she asked, hanging her elbow on the side of the stall.

Matt thumped himself in the chest with his good hand. "You're looking at him."

"*You* trained this horse?"

"None other."

She shook her head and gestured behind her at the stud. "Well, there's your option, Matt. If you can't compete, this is what you do."

"That," he said, nodding, "may have to be the plan. I've been training other horses on the side." He held up his injured hand. "That's how I got this, trying to save myself a few bucks and earn a few extra by riding a newly trained horse in a competition. If I can't rodeo, I just may have to settle for training full-time." Which meant, Neely realized, that he could do for Sheryl what she was doing now. "Thanks for your help today," he added softly. "In fact, thanks for *everything* you've done."

"No problem," she muttered, starting for the house, her heart sinking lower with every step.

Neely's glum mood bothered Matt. He'd thought she'd be pleased that he'd bullied Sheryl into having her eyes examined and new glasses ordered. He'd even driven them both into town for the appointment, his hand having improved enough for him to cut back on the pain meds. Neely had barely acknowledged the eyeglasses announcement at dinner, though. He tried to find a minute after the meal to talk to her about what was bothering her, but she made it clear that she didn't want to have a discussion. So, instead he helped Amber go over her lines for the church Christmas pageant, though how much help he was he didn't know. They joked and kidded around more than they memorized. She was playing the part of the innkeeper's wife, while Claire was playing the central character of Mary.

"Claire always gets the main part," Amber revealed innocently.

"Why does Claire always get the main part?" Matt asked, though he figured he already knew the answer.

"Because her daddy always pays for the costumes and stuff," Amber said matter-of-factly.

"That's no reason for Claire to always get the main part," Matt said.

"Miss Dench says it is."

"Who's Miss Dench?"

"She's our Sunday school teacher."

"Someone needs to have a word with Miss Dench."

"What for?"

"The book of James says that if you show favoritism, you sin."

"What's favoritism?"

"Giving somebody extra favors because they're wealthy or because you like them more than someone else."

"Miss Dench likes Mr. Wheaton," Amber said slyly.

Matt tried not to smile. "How do you know?"

Amber batted her eyelashes and said in a phony voice, "Oh, Mr. Wheaton, you're so kind and generous."

Matt laughed. "If you could remember your lines half as well as you remember gossip, we'd be done here. Maybe some cocoa will help your memory."

It didn't, though, and Neely complained on Tuesday morning that the sugar and chocolate had kept Amber awake, babbling, late into the night.

"At this rate, I'm going to have to play her part," he said. "I can't get the lines out of my head, and she can't get them into hers."

"Oh, don't let her fool you," Neely snapped. "She had them down before you ever got involved."

Matt threw up his hands. "What's with you Spence girls? One of you won't talk to me and the other one invents reasons to."

"I have work to do," Neely retorted, turning on her heel.

"So do I," he groused, snatching his hat and coat from the rack in the living room and following Neely out the door.

"Don't be ridiculous," she said, marching toward the barn. "You can't rope with that hand like it is."

"Well, somebody's got to work Blue."

She stopped and whirled to face him, an argument ready to spill out. He plunked his hat onto his head and laid a finger across her lips.

"Tell you what, I'll help you if you'll help me. Deal?" She glared at him. "Come on, Neely. What've you got to lose?"

Her nostrils flared, but then she nodded. "Fine."

Grinning, he winked at her. "That's my girl."

If looks could kill, he'd have been a withered husk. "I am not your girl." Striding off in the direction of the barn once more, she swung her arms at her sides.

No, she was not, but she wasn't Noble Wheaton's girl, either. Somehow, Matt figured God had a message in that for one of them—him, Neely or Noble. He just wasn't sure who was missing what here.

Wheaton showed up the next afternoon while they were working Blue again. Neely didn't seem to notice at first as she dismounted and ran for the dummy. Blue had figured the thing out long since and was already quivering in anticipation. She quickly released the levers and threw up her hands as the hay bale flopped over. Blue backed up, keeping tension on the rope. Neely ran and practically vaulted into the saddle. Matt counted off six seconds as he walked out to the machine and began setting it to rights. Neely walked Blue forward and flipped the loop off the head of the dummy.

"We're going to have to get you some real calves to rope," Matt told her, aware of Wheaton climbing up on the fence.

She laughed and coiled the rope as she rode Blue toward him. Matt tamped down his dislike for the man as he followed on foot.

"That is one mighty fine animal," he heard Wheaton say as he drew near.

Neely patted Blue's neck. "Matt's roping horse."

Wheaton turned his steely gaze on Matt. "You thinking of selling?"

"What would make you suppose that?" Matt asked nonchalantly.

Wheaton glanced at the bandage on his hand. "Horse like this would bring a good price."

"Not interested in selling."

"You change your mind," Wheaton said, plucking a business card from his suit coat and offering it to Matt, "you come on by my auction house."

Matt looked at the card but didn't take it. "Won't be changing my mind. Thanks all the same." He could almost hear Wheaton's back teeth grinding. He turned a sour look on Neely.

"Is my daughter's horse going to be ready for her birthday?"

Neely seemed taken aback. "Noble, I told you that the horse would be ready. Nothing's changed."

He looked down, obviously softening. "It's just that the horse is a combination birthday and Christmas present. I don't want anything to go wrong with Claire's big day."

"I'll have Amber out here working Buttercup this afternoon," Neely told him. "The horse will be ready for Claire. I promise."

He nodded, smiling. "Speaking of Amber, you know of course that the two of you are invited to the party."

Once again, Neely seemed caught off guard. "Oh, um, Amber will be thrilled, and of course she wouldn't dream of missing Claire's birthday, but I—I'll have to check my calendar."

Noble Wheaton's head did a fast swivel, and for the second time that day if glowers were lasers, Matt would have been toast. He coughed into his hand, hiding his smile.

"In that case," Noble said, "I'm glad I gave you ten days' lead time."

"Er, yes," Neely muttered. "Good thinking."

Wheaton nodded and climbed down off the fence.

"See you at midweek service tomorrow," Matt called gaily, waving.

Oops, there went that look again. Three for three.

Matt just smiled, and when they got to the church the next evening, he made very sure that he sat next to Neely. Gran went off to sit with friends in another group, her "prayer clique," she called them. Amber and Claire had their own activities apart from the adults. Matt stuck to Neely like glue, his injured hand touching the small of her back.

She wore jeans and boots tonight, but he thought she looked as womanly as she had last Sunday in her ruffled skirt and little sweater. He couldn't imagine her not looking womanly. No wonder Wheaton was after her. Half the men in the county were probably after her. In fact, Matt was puzzled why they weren't hanging around the door in droves, begging to take her out. Had Wheaton scared them all off? It seemed likely, given the frown on his face. Matt ignored him and concentrated on the service, which culminated with group prayer.

Matt put forward a couple of requests himself, one for healing, the other unspoken. He didn't want to get hopes up until he knew for sure what was possible. Neely also asked for prayer without explaining the need. He figured he knew what the problem was, but he couldn't very well say anything reassuring there at the meeting, so he looped his arm about her shoulders and tried to say it with touch. She went as still as a deer caught in headlights. He took his arm away, worried that she'd mistaken the gesture.

They didn't get out of the building after the service before his phone vibrated in his pocket. He dug it out, checked the caller ID and stepped aside to take the call. Relieved and pleased by what he heard, he turned the ringer back on and put away the phone.

"Now, that's what I call answered prayer."

"Oh?" Grandma said. "Want to share?"

"Uh, no, not just yet," he hedged. "Good news, though."

Sheryl smiled. "We can always use good news." She frowned again. "I wish that brother of yours would give me some."

Matt shrugged that off. Marcus was usually the last person Matt worried about. His little brother had always been the "good son," the one who did everything right. Wherever he was, whatever he was doing, Marcus surely would be fine. Matt counted on it.

When they reached the house, Matt behind the wheel of the truck, he reached across the cab and caught Neely's arm as Gran and Amber climbed down out of the backseat.

"I need to talk to you for a sec."

Neely frowned. "I should get Amber in the tub."

"This won't take long."

She sighed and nodded. "Go ahead. Say it and get it over with."

"I need you to drive me to the doc again on Friday morning. These stitches are finally going to come out, and I may be in too much pain to drive myself home again."

She blinked at him. "That's it? That's what you wanted to talk to me about?"

"Yeah, that's it. What'd you think?"

"I thought…" She shook her head. "No idea. Just… the doctor. Sure. No problem."

He smiled and reached up to smooth the hair away from her lovely face. "Thanks. I appreciate it. More than you know."

She opened her mouth as if to speak then closed it again, and he had the sudden, overwhelming urge to do something insane. Just as he was about to dip his head, she yanked open the door and slid down to the ground. Only then did it hit him that he'd almost kissed her. Shaken, he got out on his side and followed her into the house, deciding that he ought to keep his distance until Friday.

He still wasn't sure how things were shaping up here; how could he be when he had no way of telling what the future might hold? If his hand healed properly, what was to keep him from getting right back into competition? And either way, what would Neely want with a half-crippled cowboy, after all, when she could have a well set-up businessman like Noble Wheaton? Just because they weren't dating now didn't mean they wouldn't be. Now *that* was something to cause an idiotic dreamer like him to lose sleep.

"Morning, curly."

Neely watched Matt cover a yawn before nonchalantly dropping a kiss onto the top of Amber's head. He didn't look as if he'd slept well, and she wondered if his hand pained him more than he'd let on. She'd hardly seen him yesterday. Amber smiled up at him, hunched over her oatmeal.

"Morning."

"You miss the bus?"

"Uh-uh. You and Neely are taking me to school on the way to the doctor."

He feigned surprise, winking at Neely. "We are? Only if you've saved me some of that cinnamon toast I see over there."

"You got to eat your oatmeal first," Amber instructed. "Sis said so."

Matt turned to Neely. "That so, sis?" His dark eyes plumbed hers, searching for what she wasn't sure, but she had a difficult time not gliding closer.

"That's right. Oatmeal first. Cinnamon toast second."

He reached around her and took a bowl from the counter, never breaking his gaze from hers. "Load it up then."

Fumbling for the bowl, she turned to the range with it and then found that she had to catch her breath before she could fill it with buttery oatmeal. She must be out of her mind, going all gooey over a guy like Matt Ender.

Why, oh, why couldn't she warm up to Noble Wheaton instead? Yeah, Noble liked to throw his weight and his money around a little bit, but he was a nice enough guy, and he was certainly a devoted father. He was no Matt Ender in the looks and personality department, though, but then that was really another strike against Matt, who probably had a girl in every rodeo town he'd ever passed through. And every one of them probably had a big old aching hole in her chest where her heart used to be. Neely told herself that the best thing that could happen was for him to get well and get gone.

He ate his breakfast, including three pieces of cinnamon toast, and drove Amber to school before heading over to the doctor's office. At Matt's insistence, Neely took the truck to the mercantile to make a payment on the layaway, and while she was there, she picked up some socks and gloves and a bandanna print knit scarf for him, so he'd have a gift under the Christmas tree like everyone else. No doubt eventually Sheryl would buy something for him, but until then, he'd have this. She drove back down to the doctor's office, and when she pulled up out front in the truck, the nurse came to the window and waved her inside.

Dr. Solomon wanted to see her, it seemed. Following the nurse back to the examination room, Neely silently prayed that all was well with Matthew's hand. When she entered the small room, Matt was sitting on a chair, his forearm and hand laid atop the flat surface of a small metal examining table. Surprised to see bloodied swabs, she stepped up behind him and clasped his shoulders in a gesture of support.

"Hello, Neely," Dr. Solomon said, pulling a dark thread from the mess that was Matt's thumb. "Almost done here." Swollen and crisscrossed with swirling incisions, it looked like something out of a monster movie. A drop of blood leaked from the hole left by the stitch.

Matt tilted back his head, looking up at her. "You don't have to watch."

"Does it hurt?"

"Not right now. Doc shot it up with something to deaden it."

"I asked you to come in," Solomon said, "because he's going to need some help with bandaging."

"Looks like you're elected," Matt said apologetically. "Hope you don't mind. You can show Grandma how to do it when we get home."

Neely wanted to wrap her arms around him, pull his head close to hers and tell him that she'd do everything in her power to fix him up again, but she just nodded.

"Nurse will demonstrate while I finish," the doctor said.

The nurse took Neely's right hand in hers and began to demonstrate how to turn a latex glove inside out, cut it, slide it over Matt's thumb, lower hand and wrist, and tape it in place so he could more easily shower and bathe without soaking the injured tissue. It proved difficult with Neely's perfectly healthy hand; she could imagine how it would feel to Matt's injured one, but she would do her best for him, and it would be for only another week or so. Then, according to the doctor, Matt would have to begin physical therapy.

Matt had prescriptions to fill after the doctor had finished with him. He complained that his numbed hand felt three times its normal size, so she drove. That, after all, was why she'd come along in the first place. At the drugstore, they sat side by side at the old-fashioned soda counter and enjoyed fancy hot peppermint chocolate coffee with tiny scoops of ice cream melting in it while they waited for the pharmacist to fill the prescriptions. Then Matt wandered the aisles buying everything Christmassy he could find, from a teddy bear in a Santa hat to a crèche in a snow globe. He even bought Christmas candy, the old-fashioned ribbon kind and the chewy nougat stuff that Amber loved, as well as some specially flavored jelly beans that were sure to be a hit with Sheryl. It was all silly fun.

As they walked back to the truck with his purchases, Neely said, "I can't figure out if you're trying to get into the Christmas spirit or if you're overflowing with it."

"Overflowing," he replied, grinning. "I haven't had a real Christmas since…" He stopped, sighed and admitted, "Well, since my dad died. Gran tried. She really did, but I just couldn't…" He shook his head.

"What changed?" Neely asked. "What's different about this year?"

He looked down at his damaged hand, and she thought, *Not me, that's for sure. Not me.* Then, out of nowhere, *Say it's me.*

"I'm not sure," he said. "Maybe I just finally grew up."

She tried, so hard, not to be disappointed. Smiling, she said, "Happens to the best of us. Merry Christmas, Matt."

He ducked his head. "Merry Christmas, Neely."

Chapter Five

When they reached the truck, Matt opened the back door of the cab, tossed his purchases inside and felt around under the seat for something, finally pulling out a red cardboard tube.

"Let me show you what I'm planning." Waving her toward the truck door, he said, "Get in. Get in. It's too cold out here for this."

Going around to the driver's side, Neely climbed up into the cab. He'd already closed himself in on the passenger side and parked the tube upright between his feet.

Popping the top off with his left hand, he said, "You'll have to help me. This thumb's starting to hurt like crazy." She just looked at him, unsure until he said, "Pull it out." Reaching into the tube, she pulled out a roll of paper. "Open it up."

She unrolled the oversize sheaf of papers. It was a house plan.

"You're building a house."

"No, I'm building onto Gran's," he explained excitedly. "I had to find the original plans and get them to a buddy of mine over in Duncan, an architect, to see if it was possible, and he says it's no problem to add a couple of bedrooms and a nice big bath, maybe a little powder room under the stairs, too." He grinned. "Can't have too many bathrooms with all you women around."

Neely stared at him for a full ten seconds. "You're building onto the house."

"Well, it isn't big enough as it is. Where's Marcus going to stay when he gets here? And you want to share a bed with Amber forever? I mean, unless you're planning to move out."

She shook her head, tears suddenly clogging her throat. "No! I—I wasn't sure you'd let us stay."

"*Let* you?" He shifted in his seat, staring at her as if she'd grown a third eye. "Neely, it's not for me to *let* you do anything. What's between you and Grandma Sheryl is your business. You can't fault me for wanting to make sure she isn't being taken advantage of, but barring that, I've got no real say in who comes and who goes at the ranch."

"You know that's not true. Sheryl's told me in no uncertain terms that when she goes, the ranch belongs to you and Marcus."

"Well, last I checked, she wasn't going anywhere, and God willing she won't for a long time to come. Meanwhile, what the two of you have going is a thing to behold. I'm proud as punch of both of you."

Neely ducked her head, her throat too clogged to speak, and nodded. He clumsily rolled up the plans and shoved them back into the cardboard tube, then pushed the lid back into place.

"I want this to be a surprise, so you won't say anything to Gran. Right? I'm just going to stick a bow on this and put it under the tree. Then on Christmas Eve, I'll show her. What do you think?"

"I think she'll be thrilled," Neely said, "especially if it means both of her boys will be home more often to use those extra rooms."

Matt smiled, cradling his hand against his chest. The bandage was smaller now, but the strain around his eyes showed her that the pain was back in full force. She wanted to ask him if he would be staying on permanently once the renovations to the house were completed or if he just wanted to make sure that he had a convenient bed when he dropped in for a visit, but when he laid his seat back and pulled his hat down over his eyes, she didn't have the heart to task him further. That or she didn't have the heart to hear his answer.

Awkwardly pouring coffee with his left hand at the breakfast table on Sunday morning, Matt mentally prepared himself.

Carefully lifting the mug with his bare right hand, he sipped the hot, fragrant brew. The hand hurt like crazy, but he was doing everything the doctor had told him to do to try to regain full use.

"How is it this morning?" Neely asked, rising from her chair and carrying her plate to the sink.

"Stiff. Numb in places and still hurts like blazes."

"The physical therapy should help," she said.

He smiled. "Yeah, but I can't just sit around here waiting to get better." Before he could say more on that, Gran called from the living room.

"Let's get a move on. I want to be early this morning."

Matt took a long slurp of his coffee as he got to his feet. "Coming, Gran!"

Neely gave a little shrug and hurried out, her long velvet skirts swishing around her boot tops. He allowed himself a moment to admire how lovely she looked in the matching vest over the white ruffled blouse, her sleek, light red hair tucked into a neat roll at her nape. She was all class, Neely Spence, every inch of her special. He looked down at his mangled, now unbandaged right hand and shook his head before following her.

He drove, taking great pleasure in it, and let Gran off right at the door, beneath the drive-through. She hurried inside. He had no idea what was so important that they had to get there early, but when he, Neely and Amber walked into the nearly deserted sanctuary, they found Sheryl sitting with the pastor in prayer. He and Neely traded looks. Her small, capable hand found its way into his.

Those beautiful blue eyes stared up at him, and Matt felt his heart skip a beat. Then Amber yanked on Neely's other hand, pulling them apart.

"Can I go wait for Claire?"

"Sure, honey. No running."

Amber took off at as fast a walk as possible. Chuckling, Matt lifted an arm at a nearby pew. "Let's sit."

Neely slipped into the space ahead of him, being careful to leave enough room for Sheryl on the end. After a few minutes, Sheryl joined them. Matt lifted his left arm and wrapped it around his grandmother, hugging her close.

Smiling, she patted his knee and laid her silver head on his shoulder. Matt felt his chest swell, and once more, Neely's hand crept into his. He gripped her fingers with his, feeling the ache in his thumb and wondering why he hadn't come home more often. Why had he denied himself this closeness with his grandmother, this chance for…what? He was almost afraid to follow that thought to the end.

Amber showed up a few minutes later with Claire. Wheaton, however, sat behind them this time rather than next to his daughter. Matt could feel the man's dour gaze drilling into the back of his head, but he chuckled to himself, thinking that Wheaton didn't know much about what it took to perform in front of a rodeo crowd if he thought staring would unnerve Matt. He'd failed spectacularly before thousands and succeeded, too; one man's glower meant nothing, and if Neely was even aware of her suitor, she didn't show it. Matt tried not to think that she could be using him to make Wheaton jealous, but that wouldn't be the first time such a thing had happened. He'd never minded before, maybe because he'd never before cared about the girl using him. Did that mean he *did* care about Neely? That was a scary thought.

After the service, they found that the overcast skies had yielded to a cold, drizzly rain that would likely turn to sleet by nightfall. Matt left the ladies standing beneath the drive-through and jogged out to the truck. His hand ached deeply, but he wouldn't have his womenfolk out in this weather. When the truck got to them, they clambered up inside, "aahhing" at the warmth blowing out of the heater.

He got them home as quickly as he could and pulled the truck right up to the porch so Gran and Amber could hop out and dart under the overhang. Neely started to get out, too, but he stopped her by quickly locking the door.

"Uh-uh. Let me turn the truck around."

"Then you'll have to run around it in the rain."

"I'm wearing a hat. All that pretty hair of yours is uncovered."

She just looked at him, a smile in her eyes. He turned the truck around so she could dash onto the porch in a single step, then he ran around the vehicle in the rain, glad she waited for him so they could go into the house together.

The whole place enveloped him like a warm hug. Gran had added to the decor over the days. Now, in addition to the tree twinkling with colored lights, bulbs, garland and other sparklies, the staircase banister had been threaded with greenery and tied with bows, while the golden glow of candles lit every nook and cranny. She'd set out the nativity figurines, placing the lopsided stable that he and Marcus had built years ago out of twigs in the center of the mantel over the fireplace and arranging the little china statues that his long-dead grandpa had bought her decades before inside and around that pathetic bit of carpentry. Colorful stockings hung to each side of the fire, which Gran even now stoked to life as Amber finished lighting the candles. A big glass bowl full of ornaments too old or fragile to go on the tree sat in the center of the formal dining table in the dining area that they used only on special occasions, and a red-, white- and green-striped throw was draped over Gran's rocking chair, crocheted by her own hand, no doubt. And there, in its traditional place at the very foot of the stairs, hung a ball of mistletoe. Matt smiled, remembering how Gran used to stand at the foot of the stairs in the morning, waiting for him, Marcus and their dad to come down, demanding her kiss from each of them.

Home. He realized how desperately he had missed

it and how very happy he was to be back here again, especially for Christmas.

"I'm so glad you're home," Gran whispered, coming to stand next to him. "So glad."

"I am, too," Matt said, smiling. "Even if I had to mangle myself to get here."

She chuckled, her eyes glistening behind the lenses of her glasses. "If I'd known you'd feel that way," she teased, "I'd have prayed an injury on you a long time ago."

He grinned, but he didn't say that it wouldn't have been right if he'd come home sooner because Neely wouldn't have been here before now. He didn't say it, but he thought it.

Amber still sat at the breakfast table that next morning when a pickup truck and trailer pulled into the yard. Neely looked out the window to see a tall, beefy cowboy in a plaid wool coat crawl out of the truck cab. He slammed a black hat down onto his head and started for the kitchen door. Just then, Matt came into the room, fresh out of the shower, his wet hair plastered to his head and his right hand held out.

"Can you get this off me? Gran's got it taped on so tight I can't peel it off."

Even with her new glasses, Sheryl still didn't completely trust her own eyesight and tended to overdo some things. Neely grabbed the scissors and went to work. At the same time, a knock sounded on the kitchen door.

"Company!" Amber announced needlessly, bouncing up to throw open the door.

"Hello," said the big man behind the screen.

"Come in, Jake," Matt called, "and set yourself down."

Taking his hat in his hands, the fellow crossed over the threshold, nodding to Neely and Amber. His hand free, Matt walked over to close the door, making introductions.

"These are the Spence girls, Neely and Amber. Ladies, this is Jake Nooner. Pardon me for not shaking, Jake," Matt added, holding up his injured hand.

"Heard about what happened," Jake rumbled in a voice as deep as the Grand Canyon, looking at Matt's hand.

"Heard about your troubles in Pueblo," Matt returned.

"Think you can help me?" Jake asked.

"Let's sit down and talk about it over a cup of coffee."

While Jake shrugged out of his coat and hung it on the back of his chair and the men sat down, Neely threw away the rubber glove bandage she'd cut from Matt's hand, washed her own hands and got down two mugs, which she filled with hot coffee. His hat on the table next to him, Jake launched into a tale about an expensive but balky roping horse that had cost him dearly at more than one event.

"I plumb gave up on him after Pueblo," Jake said, sounding disgusted, "but I've got too much invested in him to give up completely. Everyone says you're a genius with training, but like I said on the phone, after what happened in Florida, if you'd rather not take this on, I'll understand."

Matt glanced at Neely. "I might need some help, but if I can get it, I'm willing."

Neely felt her heart swell. Her? Was he asking her for help?

"In fact, Jake," Matt went on, "you just might be answered prayer. Let's finish our coffee and see what we're up against."

Amber snagged Neely's hand then, whining, "Come on, sis. I'm gonna miss the bus!"

Nodding, Neely instructed her to get her stuff together and be sure to find her gloves. "Then get in the car. I'll drive you down to the road."

"Maybe you'll join us when you get back?" Matt asked as she reached for the coat and hat she'd left hanging on a peg by the kitchen door.

Neely froze then tossed him a smile over her shoulder. "Sure."

"Great," he said, "because I'm gonna need your help."

Neely shoved her arms into her coat and crammed her hat onto her head, trying not to let him see how pleased and proud that made her feel. Snagging the keys off the hook, she opened the door.

As she went out, she heard Jake, who had his back to her, say, "Now, there's a looker."

Pausing, she waited for Matt's reply. "Oh, she's more than that. Way more. Including a fine horse trainer."

Smiling, she pulled the door closed that last little bit and went to warm up the car. Maybe what Matt had said didn't mean anything. Maybe she was getting her hopes up over a cowboy who would drive off one day and never look back, but maybe, just maybe, it wouldn't hurt to pray for a chance for more.

When she returned to the house after seeing Amber onto the school bus, she found Matt and Jake in the corral with Jake's horse, a big Appaloosa crossbreed, all black in front and white with black spots in back. His name was Half-n-Half, but Jake had taken to calling him Psycho because of his behavior.

"He just won't load into the starting box," Jake complained, stepping up into the saddle to demonstrate the problem.

Sure enough, the horse swung his head wildly side to side and skittered around rather than backing straight into the box.

"Can you head him in?" Matt asked.

Jake turned the horse and rode him headfirst into the box without a problem, but then turning him and backing him into the corner proved impossible. The horse kept swinging his head, snorting and pulling around. Matt got on and tried him, but his grip on the reins wasn't as strong as he'd have liked, so he couldn't measure the strength of the horse's resistance.

"Neely, you give it a go."

She let Matt toss her up into the saddle. Both he and Jake moved to shorten the stirrups for her, but the horse was having none of it. He started flinching and dancing around. Matt pulled her down, his hands at her waist.

"Jake, hold his head," he instructed, quickly adjusting the right stirrup, but when he walked around to the left side, the horse went berserk, dancing and snorting and pulling on the reins.

Matt moved to take the reins from Jake, standing squarely in front of the animal. Talking softly and gently, he petted the horse on the right side. It calmed instantly, but when he touched it on the left, it jerked and shied.

"Jake," Matt said calmly, waving his hand in front of the horse's left eye, "this horse is blind on the left side."

Jake's mouth dropped open. "How...when...?" He

backed up half a dozen steps, yanked his hat off and beat it against his thighs, muttering some choice words. "I knew Appaloosas were prone to night blindness, but this…" He kicked a dirt clod. "I suppose he's useless now."

"Not necessarily," Matt said. "Let us get a vet out here to check him over. If everything's okay, and I expect it will be since this likely happened a while ago, we'll work with him. You come back after the first of the year, and we'll give you a little retraining, too. See if we can't make a team out of the two of you again. Until then, you just pay for expenses, like the vet, feed and board." He looked to Neely then. "That sound okay to you?"

Smiling softly, she nodded. "That sounds okay to me."

Matt patted the horse and glanced at Jake. "This works for you, then you can pay us the fee we discussed."

Shoulders slumping, Jake walked forward and wrapped his arms around the horse's neck, careful to keep on his right side. "I'm sorry, buddy," he muttered. "I shoulda known there was something wrong—shoulda gotten you help sooner."

Neely felt sure she saw tears in his eyes when he finally pulled back. "You take good care of him," he said to Matt.

"We will," Neely answered for both of them.

Matt said, "We need to get this corral disked up and sanded. It's too hard and compacted for serious training."

"I'll take care of it today," she said. "I know just who to call."

"And we're going to need some calves. That old roping machine isn't going to cut it anymore."

She pursed her lips. "I think I know a family I can barter some riding lessons to for the use of some stock."

"Told you she was more than just good-looking," Matt said as Jake took out his wallet and forked over several bills. He said it looking her straight in the eye, and she very much feared that he could see exactly how much it thrilled her.

Chapter Six

The vet couldn't say why Psycho had lost sight in the one eye, but the right seemed fine, and everything else checked out. He chalked it up to a birth defect and gave the go-ahead for training. They got the corral plowed and sanded multiple times, until it was like walking on carpet with six-inch padding.

Meanwhile, Matt set up a calf chute and a holding pen behind it. By Friday at lunchtime, Matt felt exhausted, and they hadn't even started working Jake's horse yet. He had another doctor's appointment, though, not that he minded. He felt that the work he'd done getting the corral ready had improved his grip, and his pain level had decreased significantly. He couldn't help feeling encouraged, though his mood outpaced his energy level.

"I can drive myself," he told Neely and Gran. "No one else needs to come unless they just want to."

Neely looked at Gran and said, "I still have layaway."

"Well, if you're going into town, sweetie," Gran said, "could you pick up some things at the grocery? I promised Amber we'd make fudge and sugar cookies tonight."

"No problem."

"Ooh, Gran's Christmas fudge," Matt said. "We used to give tins to all our teachers and coaches at school. Of course they were half-empty before we got them there."

"As if you didn't have plenty of it here at home!" Gran scolded good-naturedly.

"It's just so good, Gran," Matt said, grinning. This felt like a double win, Grandma Sheryl's Christmas fudge and Neely riding into town with him of her own accord.

"Maybe we can pick up Amber from school on our way home. It'll save her time on the bus and help get a head start on that Christmas cooking," Neely said. "It's the last day of school before Christmas break."

These rural bus routes could be hours long, as Matt well knew. The school district tended to reverse them year to year so the same kids didn't always have the longest rides. He nodded.

"Sounds like a plan, but we better get a move on. I heard Amber say that school gets out early today."

They hopped into his truck and sailed down the road, Neely driving to save time switching over once they reached the doctor's office. She dropped him there and headed off to take care of the layaway payments and shopping. The doctor had finished his cursory examination and walked Matt out to the waiting area just as the pickup pulled into the parking lot. A discussion about physical therapy was ongoing. Hoping to derail it, Matt waved at Neely through the window. She seemed to take that as instruction to come inside. Before he got his wallet out to pay for his visit, she pushed through the door into the common area.

"What's up?"

Dr. Solomon answered. "He's made real improvement. No more worries about soaking it, but now we have to move on to rehabilitation. He's got diagrammed exercise sheets with detailed explanations of how to begin using that thumb, but the therapeutic massage is extremely important because of the amount of scar tissue."

"I get that, Doc," Matt said, trying not to snap. "All I'm saying is that three or four trips a day to the rehab center in Lawton is not an option. I'm sure Gran will agree to be trained for it if you'll just get the therapist over here."

"Is tomorrow too soon?" Solomon asked.

"I'll have to talk to her," Matt began, but to his surprise, Neely stepped up.

"I'll do it."

Matt blinked at her. Before he could say anything, Solomon spoke again. "You'd be the better option. Young hands tend to be stronger hands."

"Don't you have plans for tomorrow?" Matt asked, thinking of Claire Wheaton's birthday party.

She shook her head. "I never committed to anything."

Matt stepped close and softly said, "I appreciate this, Neely, but we're not talking about training a horse for half the fee."

She pressed her lips together, glaring at him. "I know that."

Matthew wanted to hug her. Instead he whispered, "It's a mighty big favor, girl."

"I'm not some silly girl," she hissed.

"I sure know *that*."

She dropped her gaze then looked at Dr. Solomon. "Tomorrow will be fine."

"I'll set it up." He shook his finger at Matt then, saying, "Now, you do like I told you about those gloves."

Matt nodded, sighing. "All right."

As they exited the building, Neely asked what the deal was with the gloves.

Matt held up his hands. "Seems my right hand is now significantly larger than my left and may well be from now on, so I have to buy two different sizes of work gloves."

"After what happened with your glove getting caught in the dally, I'm surprised you'd even agree to wear them again," Neely exclaimed.

"That glove is the only reason I have a thumb," Matt told her. "If I hadn't been wearing it, the rope would've taken my thumb off completely and mangled the tissue to the point of no recovery."

"Well, let's get you properly outfitted then," she said adamantly.

"What about Amber?"

"If we hurry, we can still catch her. If not…" Neely shrugged. "This is more important. You can't be working that Appaloosa without properly fitting gloves."

Matt smiled and nodded. A fellow could get real fond of a woman like Neely Spence. If he was of a mind to turn his whole life upside down in order to stay in one place beside her. But then, hadn't his life already been upended? He made as tight a fist as he could with his right hand, wondering if God was trying to tell him something.

They hurried at the mercantile, but by the time they

got to the school, the buses were already pulling out of the lot. The driver stopped to let Amber off, anyway.

"One of the pluses of a small school in a small town," Neely told Matt. "Here where everybody knows everybody else, it's no big deal."

"Never thought about it," Matt admitted. "Education was not so important to me because I always knew I was going to rodeo, but my brother has done well coming out of this small school in a small town. He's actually got multiple degrees."

"Yeah, your grandma's told me," Neely said as Amber ran toward the pickup. "Have you never thought of doing anything else except rodeo?" she asked.

"No," he answered simply, because really he never had.

Oh, in the back of his mind he'd always known that the day would come when he'd have to do something else. Rodeo was a young man's game. He'd had lots of jobs along the way; a fellow had to eat until he could figure out how to earn a living at this rodeo business and make a name for himself. Matt had always figured that he'd fall back on something he'd picked up, like horse training, maybe. But lots of cowboys competed with multiple injuries. He might be able to adjust. If he wanted to.

He'd been awfully close to the big time this year. If he'd been able to compete in the finals, he actually might have won. Or not. Could be he'd never know. If he gave up, he certainly wouldn't. Surely he didn't have to explain all that to Neely, though. She'd been there.

She'd been there and given it up to raise her baby sister. Social services would have taken Amber if Neely hadn't, but Neely had stepped up and shouldered the task. He knew without even having to ask that she didn't have a single regret about that, either. He saw the quiet way Neely loved on that girl. He saw, too, how happy Amber was. Neely had given her that.

They drove back to the ranch with Amber's excited chatter filling the cab of the pickup. She couldn't wait to make fudge and bake cookies with Grandma Sheryl or attend Claire's birthday party. Having saved the princely sum of eleven dollars and sixty-two cents, she'd made Sheryl promise to take her Christmas shopping, and could they please drive to Lawton to look at the Christmas lights one night? Mr. Wheaton had taken Claire, and she said the lights were "way cool." Amber wanted to wrap Claire's birthday present in blue because Claire didn't like it when her birthday presents looked like her Christmas presents.

When they pulled into the yard, they found Noble Wheaton's luxury sedan there, accompanied by a pickup truck and horse trailer painted with his daughter's name, as if she was already a prize-winning barrel racer. Matt just shook his head. Neely killed the engine and handed him the key fob, following Amber, who was halfway to Wheaton's car before Neely's boots hit the ground. Sighing, Matt got out, gathered up the purchases and carried them into the house before joining the others outside.

Neely already had Buttercup on a lead and halfway across the yard by the time he reached the trailer. The hired hand with the trailer gave him a nod, but Wheaton completely ignored Matt. He didn't mind. He stood aside and let Neely do her thing.

When the horse was loaded, Neely smiled at Wheaton and said, "As soon as Claire is ready, I am. Christmas vacation might be a good time to get started with her training."

"Uh, yes," Wheaton hedged. "Perhaps you could discuss it with her in detail at the party tomorrow."

"Oh, I'm sorry," Neely said smoothly. "I have another commitment."

Wheaton stiffened. "I see."

"But of course Amber wouldn't miss it, and I'll see to it that she gets there."

"I'll be happy to bring her home afterward if that will help," Wheaton offered.

Neely smiled. "That would be very helpful. Thank you."

"My pleasure," he told her, clasping her hand.

Neely stepped back, pulling her hand free. Wheaton gave whispered directions to the hired hand then got into his car. The truck and trailer rig pulled out of the yard with Wheaton's sedan following closely behind. Amber waved and ran into the house. As composed as ever, Neely turned to follow, but Matt reached out with both hands to stop her. He wondered if she realized that she'd just put him ahead of Noble Wheaton. One look into her big blue eyes told her that she did.

"Thank you," he said, wondering if he was worth it. She just looked at him, giving away nothing, and suddenly simple thanks was not enough. He wrapped his arms around her, stepping close, and hugged her. "Thank you."

She briefly laid her head on his shoulder. Then she turned and walked into the house.

On their way to the appointment with the physical therapist at Solomon's office the next morning, they dropped Amber off at the Wheaton place on the outskirts of Red Bluff. Matt couldn't help a spurt of envy when he turned the pickup into the long drive. The house was a palace, the outbuildings and pens as neat and organized as a surgical suite, the fields and yard strangely lush for winter. The place was devoid of Christmas decorations, however, and awash with blue and yellow birthday banners and streamers. Half the county appeared to have been invited.

"What is it that Wheaton does again?" Matt asked.

"He owns several livestock auction barns," Neely said, "and other things. Oil leases, I think, and…" She shook her head.

Matt looked around. "Does he ranch?"

"He owns land and raises some fodder, but I'm not sure he actually ranches."

"Have you been here before?"

"Sure," she answered, "several times."

The truck reached the apex of the circular drive at the end of the long, straight road leading to it. Matt put the transmission in Park, and Neely slid out to hug Amber and make sure she had the card that went with the gift she carried.

"See you later, sweetie."

"Bye!"

Neely climbed back up into the cab and buckled her seat belt. "Better move it, cowboy. Don't want to be late."

Matt shifted and hit the gas pedal, but he couldn't help glancing into his rearview mirror as he wheeled the truck away from the house.

"This is quite a place."

"It's nothing compared to where I grew up," Neely told him quietly.

Matt shot her a surprised glance. "How so?"

She settled back in her seat as if deciding just how much to tell him. "Eight thousand square feet," she said, "marble floors, cook, maids, gardeners. Nannies."

"Neely!" Matt exclaimed, shocked.

"I grew up outside of Tulsa," she went on. "Rich, pampered only child until Amber came along. Mom's little accident." She shook her head. "They didn't really have time for either one of us. The only reality, the only people with genuine love for me in my life were my mom's parents here in Red Bluff. Solid, Christian people, salt of the earth. They died years before my folks did, so Amber didn't really have a chance to know them. But after we lost everything, I brought Amber here because this was where I'd been happiest. I needed to find a way to give her the same kind of solid ground I hadn't even realized they'd given me until I needed it most." She nodded emphatically. "It was the right thing to do. I met Sheryl here."

Matt could identify with what she'd said about a solid grounding she hadn't even realized she'd received until she'd reached the end of her rope. He'd been there, more than once. When he'd gotten to that place where he'd felt beaten and lost, he'd turned to the only place he'd known to go. He had his dad and Grandma Sheryl to thank for that, which made him wonder why it had taken him so long to just come back home for more than a two-hour visit. Still…

"The Ender place doesn't compare to Wheaton's, though," Matt argued with a shake of his head.

"You're right," she said. "The Ender place is a real

home. Nothing about it is for show or meant to impress. It's a safe place in the storm, a haven of love and light. I wouldn't trade it for anything."

She wouldn't trade it for anything, but *he* had, Matt realized. He'd traded his home and all it represented for a lonely, vagabond lifestyle that had left him injured and with little to call his own. He wondered what else he'd traded away and for what and if it was too late to really come back home again. After all, what right did he have to cut himself in on Gran and Neely's deal?

The ranch had become a paying concern again because of Neely. She'd made a home in the place he'd abandoned. What right did he have to crowd her? If he could go back out onto the rodeo circuit, win some big money and invest that in the ranch, then he'd have a right to move in on what she had going here. Until then, so far as he could see, all he had was visitation rights.

What if he couldn't rodeo again, though, ever? That still didn't give him the right to move in on her. Sure, Grandma said the ranch would be partly his someday, but he hoped that wouldn't happen for a very long time. Until then, he'd just have to figure out something. Maybe if he found a solution that let him come back a little more often Neely would…what?

He couldn't let himself think what he was thinking. Somehow, though, he couldn't stop thinking it, either.

"This is for you," Noble said when he brought Amber home that evening, "a little token of my esteem."

If this two-foot-long box was a "little token" then Neely didn't want to see a full-blown expression of his feelings. Momentarily too stunned to do more than juggle the beautifully wrapped box, she glanced away as Amber slipped through the front door into the house.

"You…didn't have to do this," she babbled, belatedly finding her tongue.

Noble smiled. "Save it for Christmas, now, you hear?" He doffed his hat then turned and sauntered across the porch, light on his feet for such a solidly built man.

Neely stared at the gift in her hands with dismay. When she turned from the door, nudging it closed with her elbow, she found Matt there, his arms akimbo, thumbs hooked into the rims of the front pockets of his jeans. She didn't know how he could do that; her own hands were sore from the workout they'd gone through with the physical therapist earlier. His thumb had to be aching.

"Didn't think he was going to back off completely, did you?" he asked. "Give up without a fight? I wouldn't."

She'd tried so hard to pretend that Noble wasn't as intensely interested as he'd first seemed, that his interest had waned as she'd stalled. His possessiveness made her uncomfortable, and she really didn't want to talk about it, especially not with Matt.

"I don't know what you mean."

"Come on, Neely." Matt stepped closer, pitched his voice low, just in case Amber or Sheryl could hear him over Amber's happy chatter in the kitchen, where she'd gone to report the day's activities. "The guy's in love with you."

Neely shook her head vehemently. "You don't know that."

"Sure I do. I recognize all the signs. The way he looks at you, the way he's compelled to touch you at times, the tone of his voice when he speaks to you, how he looks at me because I'm here with you and he isn't. Now this." He nodded at the box. "You're going to find something expensive and personal in there, chosen just for you. And if you keep it, even for the next few days until Christmas, he's going to take that as a sign that you're at least tempted to take him on along with what he can give you."

"I'm not," she said, without meaning to, which surprised her because Neely had been taught to think very carefully before speaking. Her parents had appeared glib and sociable, but they were all about business and proper appearance, and a daughter who couldn't be as glib and intentional had been expected to simply smile, look pretty and be quiet. She had pretty much mastered quiet. Now that her feelings on the matter were out, though, she saw no reason not to confirm them. She lifted the box. "I was always going to give it back."

"Don't you even want to know what's inside it first?" Matt asked.

She started to shake her head. It seemed important to him, though, that she see the gift before refusing it. Uncertain why that should be so, she nevertheless carried the box to the dining table at the end of the living area and looked it over. The elaborate bow had been made and tied on after the ribbons were crisscrossed and taped onto the box. She carefully untied the bow. It came off in a single, fluffy piece, which she laid aside. Next she picked apart the tape holding the flat ribbon to the box. Once that was removed, slitting the remaining tape and unfolding the paper required only seconds.

Neely lifted off the pure white box top and spread the tissue paper beneath to reveal layers of rich blue silk. Using her fingertips, she grasped the garment by the shoulder seams and lifted it.

"Wow," Matt said. "Old Noble's got good taste. I'll give him that. Matches your eyes exactly. Looks like a perfect fit."

The label told Neely that Noble had spent hundreds on this single dress. She let it slither back into the box. "This is way too expensive and way too personal."

Matt tilted his head in a kind of shrug. "Well, he can afford it, and his feelings *are* personal."

"I'll take it back to him tomorrow."

"Eh, better let it wait until Wednesday and the mid-week service, but do it in private. That way he gets the message but doesn't have you too much to himself, the way he would if you went to his home."

"Private but not too private."

Matt nodded. "I can always be standing by, just in case, if you like."

She pulled in a deep breath. She'd like more than that, but he'd have to figure that out for himself. She wasn't about to ask him to give up his dream for her. If he could rope competitively again and that was what he wanted, then that was what she wanted for him, but what she hoped… A smart woman wouldn't even go there, no matter how hard she had to fight the urge.

Working quickly but carefully, she rewrapped the package, Matt standing at her elbow.

"You're sure about this?" he asked softly as she tied the bow back into place.

"Yes."

"You're not likely to get any other gifts like this one," he pointed out.

"It's not the gift that matters," she said in a near whisper, fluffing the bow, "as much as the giver."

He stopped her, grasping her hands and tugging her around to face him. His brown eyes drilled down into hers.

"Does it matter," he asked softly, "that I'm glad you're sending back that beautiful dress?"

She stared at him, thinking that she shouldn't lay out her heart for him, that she was making it too easy for him to use her vulnerability to hurt her, but she couldn't lie.

"Yes."

He squinted at her as if trying to read her mind, then he reached up with his right hand and swept her hair away from her face before spearing his fingers into it. She didn't have an instant to react before he closed his eyes and kissed her right on the lips, softly, gently, tenderly, almost with reverence.

Then he grinned and drawled, "I'll try to find a gift more to your liking."

Infuriating man. Hadn't she just said that it wasn't the gift that mattered but the giver?

On the other hand, how stupid would she be to discourage him from trying to please her?

She laughed softly and shook her head, knowing that she was going to replay that kiss in her mind dozens of times daily until he either gave her something else to think about or broke her heart into a million little pieces.

Chapter Seven

Neely handed Matt the special delivery letter. The mailman had driven all the way up to the house to get a signature for it, and because she'd been walking from the house to the corral, where they'd been working Jake's horse for the past two days, she'd done the honors, though the letter was addressed to Matthew E. Ender. Frowning, he used his pocketknife to slit open the envelope and extract the papers inside.

"What's the *E* for?" she asked as he scanned the first sheet.

"Hmm?"

"The *E*. What's your middle name?"

"Eric."

"Oh. Great name."

He stuffed the letter into his pocket. "I'm named after my dad. My brother and I both are. He was Eric Marcus."

"That's nice. You'll have to use Eric for your son one day."

He shot her an indecipherable look before pulling off his hat and rubbing the top of his head, which made her laugh.

"Why do you do that? You do that all the time."

"What?"

"Rub the top of your head."

He smiled sheepishly. "Uh, I don't know. I guess…" He shrugged. "My dad used to do that all the time. After he died, I guess I started doing it for myself."

She reached over with her left hand and lifted off his hat then rubbed the top of his head with her right. He chuckled.

"Thanks."

Clapping the hat back onto his head, she asked, "Want to tell me what's in the letter?"

He repositioned his hat, grinning broadly. "This year's new championship roper wants to buy my horse."

Neely staggered back a step. They'd watched the finals on the television in the evenings, and the commentators had gone on and on about how long the winning roper and his horse had worked together.

"He wants to buy Blue?"

Matt nodded. "He's retiring his animal, and I guess he figures I won't be getting back into competition after my injury, so he's made a formal offer."

"How much?"

"He opened at thirty-five K."

"Thirty-five thousand dollars?"

"Yep."

She felt absurdly proud, but was still compelled to say, "Blue's worth more."

"I think so."

"Will he pay more?"

"Yeah. Yeah, I think he will, or he would if I was going to sell, but I'm not."

Her heart *thunked*. So that was it. Matt was going

back out on the circuit. He was determined to rodeo again, come what may, even if his hand wasn't up to it, even if he failed spectacularly. He just couldn't give it up. Well, it was only what she'd expected, even if it disappointed.

Then Matt said, "What I'm going to do is breed up some little Blues and train them."

Neely caught her breath. "Seriously?"

"Why not? Isn't that your business model?"

She didn't bother answering that. Instead she said, "I happen to have a sturdy but speedy mare that I've held off offering to Blaze because she feels too big for a barrel racer. She seems a good match for a roping horse, though. I've got her in a batch with some other mares."

Ropers tended to be big men, bigger than the bull riders and bareback riders who benefited from a lower center of gravity and shorter limbs. Barrel racers, on the other hand, being female, often, but not always, favored smaller horses. What counted most, either way, was speed and trainability.

"Let's take a look at that mare when we're done here," Matt proposed. "If she seems likely and takes, we can train the result together and split the sale when it eventually comes."

A good roping horse out of Blue might not bring thirty-five thousand dollars initially, not unproven, but all Matt would have to do was offer to loan the horse to a top contender and let the results set the price. Or he could go out and rope on that newly trained horse himself. This was a several-years-long project, though, and the idea that he was planning to stick around that long sounded like a sort of permanence to Neely. Of course, in the meantime, Matt could hit the road again, traveling from rodeo to rodeo. Even if he made the ranch his base of operations, he could spend from a few days a year to a few days a week here, but it was better than nothing.

She put out her hand and felt the strength in Matt's grasp when he shook it. She felt recovery in his grip and sensed that he was going to rope again, which, she very much feared, meant that he was going to leave her. All she could do now was pray that it wouldn't be forever.

Meanwhile, she had the Christmas season to enjoy. That meant slipping into town on her own to make the final payment on the layaway and sneaking the gifts back to the house—or trying to. Matt caught her as she tiptoed across the living room on Wednesday morning.

"Where do you think you're going?"

Gasping, she jerked around to find him sitting on the couch, pulling on his boots.

"Shh. I left Amber sleeping. I need to get out of here without her."

He tugged down his pants leg, stood and walked over to the coat tree. "Let's go, then. I'll buy you breakfast."

She shook her head, but then she grabbed her coat, shrugging it on as they stepped out onto the porch. "I have to take the car so I can hide Amber's Santa gifts in the trunk."

"We can do better than that," Matt said. "Grandma had me clean out a bin in the barn and sneak some plastic tubs out there so the mice won't be tempted to nibble before Santa can deliver. She also gave me some big black plastic bags to stash the loot in just in case we're seen unloading."

Neely tugged her striped knit cap down over her ears. "God bless that woman."

"Couldn't agree more."

"I know it's silly. Amber has all but told me she never really believed in Santa. Still, it's the tradition of the thing, you know?"

"I hear you. She's been through enough. Why not give her a traditional Christmas if you can? By next year she'll probably be wanting to pick out everything herself."

"I did that one year," Neely admitted. "Mom decided I was old enough to forget the Santa thing. She gave me cash, told me to buy what I wanted. I had the driver take me to town, bought my own gifts, wrapped them and put them under the tree. Then I opened them for my parents on Christmas morning. They approved of my good taste."

Matt shook his head. "From the way Gran talked, I thought they were very loving parents who couldn't miss your races and died trying to get there."

"They loved me," she said, "but it was very important to them that their daughter be the best, the national champion. You think Noble's gone overboard with Claire, and maybe he has, but that's nothing compared to what they did for me. The only difference is, I love horses. I love to ride. I'm not sure about Claire. She isn't exactly rushing over here to learn barrel racing. At least she's not a trophy that Noble uses to close a business deal."

"Your parents did something right, Neely," Matt said. "Look at you."

She smiled, but then her stomach growled, and she quipped, "Guess we can take time for some breakfast, after all."

He laughed. "Red Bluff Café?"

"Is there someplace else?"

"Home," he answered succinctly.

Home, Neely thought. Did he really think of this place as home now?

They drove into town and parked down the block from the café. Apparently half the town breakfasted at the Red Bluff Café on Wednesday mornings. They had to settle for stools at the bar, the tables and booths being occupied by ranchers, drillers and local business-people. Cups of coffee appeared unordered, followed by a basket of biscuits and a squeeze bottle of honey. The finish had worn off the countertop and the fixed stool could definitely use some padding, but the brew and the biscuits tasted great. A few minutes after they arrived, the harried, middle-aged waitress stopped long enough to take their orders. Matt went for steak and eggs with gravy. Neely had a slice of ham, which she cut into pieces and ate with the biscuits and honey.

All around them the hum of conversation almost drowned out the Christmas music piped from a radio somewhere in the back—almost, but not quite. Decorations as faded as they were cheesy filled every nook and cranny, from the ancient silver tinsel tree in the front corner by the door to the red-and-green construction paper chain hanging in loops from the ceiling, but Matt seemed to enjoy them.

"I think these are the same decorations they had in here when I was a boy."

The older man on his left turned his head to look Matt over at that. Stacking his forearms on the counter-top, he furrowed his brow. "Don't I know you?"

"Could be. Matthew Ender."

"You're Eric Ender's boy."

Matt nodded. "Yes, sir. The oldest."

The man turned on his stool, one elbow braced on the counter. "Been following your career. Thought I'd see you at the national finals this year."

Matt held up his hand. "Had a little disagreement with a dally rope."

"That's too bad." The man frowned, shifting as the waitress slapped down his check.

"I don't know about that," Matt said, sliding a smile to Neely. "Seems to me the Lord has a way of working these things out for the good."

The man slid to his feet, picking up the check with one hand and clapping Matt on the shoulder with the others. "That sounds like your dad."

"Thank you," Matt said as the man moved away. He looked down at his plate, then his hand found Neely's and squeezed it.

The cash register rang, and the man called out, "Merry Christmas!"

Matt lifted his head, smiling. "Merry Christmas."

They sat in silence, nursing refills, until finally Matt waved at the waitress. "Check, please."

"Oh, hon, Walt Goddard paid for y'all."

"That was Walt Goddard?" Walt Goddard was a roping legend. Neely knew he lived around there, but she'd never met him. "He was my dad's best friend," Matt said, "and I didn't even recognize him."

"Walt's been ill," the waitress paused long enough to say, "and his wife and daughter both died in the last few years. Hard times."

Matt stared out the door that Goddard had gone through. "Thanks for telling me," he muttered, pulling a generous tip out of his pocket and tossing it onto the counter.

"Merry Christmas, hon!" she called as he towed Neely out of there.

"Walt Goddard has followed my career," Matt said as soon as they hit the sidewalk. He clapped a hand to the nape of his neck, grinning. "I am one dumb so-and-so. You know that? All this time, with my dad gone, I've thought there was nothing and nobody here for me except Grandma Sheryl, but there's no telling how much support I could've had if I'd just known."

Neely looped her arm through his, already feeling him slip away from her. He was going back out to rodeo. She could see it coming, as sure as rain.

"Why didn't I get back home before this?" he asked. Then he laid his hand over hers and said, "Never mind. I know why." He laughed and tugged her toward the mercantile, saying, "We have gifts to get. And to return. And to be thankful for."

She laughed with him, but she wasn't feeling terribly thankful just then. She was feeling like a woman in love with a man destined to leave her.

Noble was not happy when Neely returned his gift. Matt stood well back, giving her plenty of room to take care of things. He couldn't hear what she said, but he saw the hateful look that Noble sent his way, and it made him absolutely giddy. Even if he wasn't the reason she'd given Noble his walking papers, she'd essentially entered into partnership with him, and Matt intended to use that to his advantage. He knew where he belonged and exactly what he wanted now, and having Noble Wheaton out of the way suited him to a tee.

Watching that beautiful woman turn and walk toward him across the church parking lot, Matt felt his chest expand. That had been happening quite a bit lately, such as this morning when Walt had told him how like his dad he'd sounded and when he'd gotten that offer for Blue yesterday. It had happened when Grandma Sheryl had told him how happy she was to have him home, too, and when Amber teased him until he tickled her with his whiskers. It happened most often though when Neely looked at him with those big blue eyes of hers, that slight smile on her full, pink lips, silent pride shining out of her as they worked. Sometimes he worried that he imagined that, but he couldn't really believe it.

She slipped her arm through his, and they turned toward the truck. He thought about asking how Wheaton had taken the return of the gift, but he didn't really want to talk about Noble Wheaton anymore, so instead he asked, "Do you know who owns the hundred and sixty acres north of us?"

She thought. "Um, Stewart, I think the name is."

"That's Walt Goddard's son-in-law. Walt gave that piece of property to Stewart and his daughter when they married. She died a while ago. Now Stewart's getting married again, and Walt's buying the property back. I called Walt to thank him for paying for our breakfast, and he told me all about it."

"What does that mean for us?" Neely asked.

"Don't know yet. Walt's interested in some top-end roping horses, though."

"Interested in?"

"Owning them, leasing them out to ropers. He's talking about a delivery operation, making sure the horses get where they need to be so the roper just has to show up, practice and compete."

"Lots of cowboys can't afford to buy top-end horses," she mused. "They might be able to lease them, though."

Matt grinned. "Yep. Walt said something about forming a syndicate."

He could almost see the wheels turning in her head. "That's a different business model, Matt."

"Yep."

"I hope you're not counting on me to run it on top of the work I already have."

"Not alone." She blinked at that. "Look, it's just something to think about for now," he said.

Neely nodded, and he opened the front passenger side door of the truck cab for her. He hoped that once she had time to think it over, she'd get as excited about the possibilities as he was. He hoped for a lot of things over time.

Neither of them discussed the matter in front of Sheryl and Amber, though. Amber was busting-at-the-seams excited about Christmas. She'd performed her role in the pageant that evening perfectly. Matt teased her about where in the Bible he could find the verses telling how the innkeeper's wife had led Mary and Joseph to the stable and suggested they use the manger for a baby bed.

"Okay, we made that up," she admitted, "but there weren't enough parts for everyone, and we had more girls than boys. The important thing is that Baby Jesus was born just the way the Old Testament said He would be."

"You're sure about that?"

"Positive! Weren't you listening? I'll show you exactly where it says it in the Bible."

"I'll hold you to that," he said.

Back at the house, Amber ran upstairs to get her Bible and find her copy of the play script.

In her absence, Matt voiced his concerns about his brother. "I don't understand why Marcus hasn't arrived. Gran, tell me where Marcus last was and exactly where he was going."

Matt soon learned that his brother had been dispatched to Colorado to pick up some unusual horses that Gran wanted to raise. Neely clearly had little to no knowledge of the scheme, but at least Matt now knew where Marcus had been heading. While Amber ran upstairs to read, he got on the computer and started researching the route Marcus would have to have taken. Then he stumbled across the likely problem.

"Look at this," he said, pulling up a satellite photo of the area where Marcus had gone. "Seems to me they're snowed in up there."

Gran clapped a hand over her mouth. "Oh no. This is all my fault."

"You don't control the weather," Neely pointed out.

Matt checked the weather for the time Marcus should have arrived and saw that, while nothing major had been predicted, a freak storm had closed roads and knocked out services in the area around that time.

"The phones must be down," Gran said. "I have been calling, but no one's answered."

"What about cell coverage?" Neely asked.

Matt checked on all the major providers before shaking his head. "Man, I don't see any." He pulled up the satellite photo again, zooming in as close as he could. "Does that look like his truck? I don't even know what he's driving now."

"I'm not sure," Gran said, squinting at the screen.

"Maybe, but with everything buried in snow, who can tell?"

"We just have to trust that it is," Neely said, "and that everything is fine."

"That's snow country," Matt said. "They'd be prepared for something like this up there."

"Oh, I pray so," Gran whispered.

"We'll all pray for him," Neely told her.

"Here," Matt said, getting up from the desk and moving to the table. "We'll do it now." He pulled out a chair for Gran. She practically fell into it. Leaving a chair in the middle for himself, he pulled out another chair for Neely. Smiling at him, she slipped into it. He sat and opened his hands on the tabletop. Gran grasped his left hand with both of hers. Neely slid her hands into his wounded right one. He folded his fingers over both and closed his eyes. The sweetest sense of belonging came over him.

"Lord," he said, "You know Marcus because he belongs to You, and You love him even more than we do. All we ask is that You keep him safe and warm and get him home to us healthy and happy as soon as You can. He deserves it. I'm real proud to say that, as much as anyone does, Marcus deserves Your protection and blessing. He's always tried to do the right thing. So, we're just going to trust You to take care of him."

Both Gran and Neely whispered prayers, too, before they all said, "Amen."

"He's okay," Matt assured Gran. She stood and hugged him, her wiry arms tight about his neck.

Amber appeared just then, Bible in one hand, pageant script in the other.

"Well, are you coming?" she demanded.

"On my way," Matt promised.

Blinking, Neely got up and hurried Amber from the room. With a last hug for Grandma, Matt followed. He sat on the couch with Amber while she went through, verse by verse, proving her point.

"Now, that," Matt said proudly, experiencing another one of those chest-expanding moments, "is Christmas right there. Guess we're all done."

"But we haven't even had our gifts yet," Amber argued, suddenly panicked.

"We've had the most important one," Sheryl said. "The others are just to remind us of the gift of Christ."

"And each other," Neely added.

"That's right," Matt said. "Jesus and family. Now, that's Christmas." He didn't even remember until after he'd said it that Neely and Amber weren't family, not really. That seemed wrong. Ten kinds of wrong. And, sadly, he wasn't sure that he could make it right, but he wanted to.

He had already made a private shopping trip, but Neely didn't know that. Over the past weeks, he'd learned to read Neely pretty well. She'd seemed silent and blank at first, but it was all there in her eyes when he looked deeply enough. She was upset. She didn't let it get in the way of the work, though.

They were in the barn later, currying and feeding Psycho when Matt finally blurted, "I didn't mean to upset you."

She shot him a look filled with deadly icicles. "What makes you think I'm upset?"

"The arctic cold front that just swept through here."

Dropping her ice blue gaze, she went back to currying the hide off poor Psycho. "You will tell me before you go for good, won't you?"

"What makes you think I'm going for good?"

"Everything."

Well, *that* waxed his ears, especially after everything he'd prayed for and done and decided and...feared.

"Yeah," he snapped. "I'll let you know in dead-certain terms when I'm going for good."

"That's all I ask," she muttered, dropping the curry brush into the bucket as she marched out of the barn.

He shook his head. Did she really think he'd go without telling her? Fool woman. Did she really think he'd go unless she *made* him? Maybe that's what this was leading up to—and maybe that wasn't the problem at all.

Whipping off his hat, he rubbed the top of his head and smiled at the memory of Neely doing the same thing. Maybe, just maybe, that was the exact opposite of the problem. He didn't know which prospect scared him more, that she wanted him to go or that she wanted him to stay. He only knew that he hated it when she was mad at him.

Thankfully, by the time he went in to dinner, Neely had softened. The Christmas spirit permeated the whole house. Like a living entity, it enveloped them all in a warm, fragrant hug. She and Grandma had prepared a lovely meal with lots of goodies, which they ate at the formal dining table on Great-Grandma Ender's antique china, the fireplace in the living area across the way crackling cheerfully.

Gran had gotten out the phonograph and some records, which tickled Amber endlessly. She kept lifting the needle and setting it down again, but after the meal,

Neely convinced her to let some of the traditional carols play through so they could sing along.

Finally, Matt rubbed his hands together and said, "Well, we've got some cleaning up to do, and cookies to put out for Santa, and…" He chucked Amber under the chin. "I thought there was a special on TV you wanted to watch."

She glanced at the clock, gasped and ran for the living room. He chuckled.

"Why is Christmas so much more fun when there's a kid around?"

"I don't know, but it is," Grandma said. "How about we let the dishes go until later?"

"How about you and Amber watch the show while I clean up?" Neely said.

"We," Matt corrected. "Neely and I will take care of it. You go enjoy the program."

Gran looked at the two of them, patted a shoulder on each and said, "I'll just take you up on that. Then we've got to start for church."

"Better get to work," Neely said.

"Seems to be what we're best at," Matt muttered.

"Is that such a bad thing?" she asked.

"No. Unless you want something more."

"What do you want, Matt?"

"More," he answered succinctly. "Don't you?"

"Yes," she said. Then she went into the dining room and began clearing the table.

They barely made it, stacking the last dish just as Gran came into the room with their coats. "Come on, now. We can't miss the Christmas Eve service."

Matt helped Neely into her jacket and tossed on his

duster. Gran grabbed a tin of fudge for the pastor. Matt took it back and replaced it with another.

"I filched out of that one."

"Oh, you."

"It's just so good, Gran."

Amber jabbered excitedly about getting to go to the late Christmas Eve service, even though Claire's father had insisted that they attend the early one. Matt remembered attending the late service as a boy. They'd even gone in their pajamas at times. The reverent, candlelit ceremony had both quelled and heightened the anticipation for Christmas morning, and more often than not, they'd fallen asleep on the drive home. Amber didn't fall asleep, but she was yawning widely when they pulled up into the yard at the house.

"Straight upstairs," Neely ordered, taking off her coat. "I'm right behind you."

Amber immediately began to whine. "Couldn't I just—"

"Nope. Right to bed. It's late, and if I know you, you'll be up at dawn. Now, say good-night and go."

The girl went to Gran, hugging her around the shoulders. "Good night, Sheryl. I love you."

"Good night, Amber. Love you, too."

She came to Matt, hugging him around the waist. "Good night, Matt. Love you."

"Good night, curly. I love you, too, and hey, you know what? You're the best Christmas gift I've gotten so far this year."

She gave him another squeeze, grinning, and said, "Wait until you see what Sheryl got you."

Matt frowned. "She better not have gotten me anything."

"Oh, it's nothing much," Sheryl insisted, shooing Amber toward the stairs. "Up you go, sugar. Sleep well."

Amber scampered up the stairs. Neely laid a hand on Matt's chest, whispering, "You want to start bringing stuff in from the barn?"

"On it," he promised.

"Be down in a few minutes."

He nodded and headed outside as soon as he heard Amber's bedroom door close. Gran had conveniently disappeared.

By the time he'd hauled Amber's gifts in from the barn, Neely had a mug of hot apple cider ready for him, along with several pieces of Gran's Christmas fudge.

"If I eat all this, I'll be sick," he said. She just lifted an eyebrow. "Okay, you got me. I have a terrible sweet tooth. I've heard it's that alcoholic gene."

She tilted her head. "Are you telling me that you're an alcoholic, Matt?"

"No. I don't drink. Never wanted to. Because my mother's an alcoholic."

He waited tensely until Neely smiled.

"Merry Christmas, Matt."

"So far so good."

Matt and Neely finished their snack and went in to put out Amber's Santa gifts. They nibbled the cookies, crumbled the rest and poured out the milk. Then Neely started up the stairs.

"Good night, Matt, and thanks."

"Whoa," he said, coming to the foot of the stairs. "You can't stop there and then just go on your merry way."

Her slender brows crashed together. "What?"

He pointed upward at the mistletoe hanging overhead. She rolled her eyes, but when he butted his toes against the step on which she stood, she slid her arms around his neck. Looping his arms around her waist, he pulled her into him and brought her lips to his, feeling her breath fan against his cheek. He'd never felt anything like this, the rightness and wonder, the hope and the joy—the almost paralyzing terror.

After a long, lovely interlude, Neely broke the kiss. She smiled, then she reached up and rubbed the top of his head before practically skipping up the stairs.

Chuckling, Matthew dropped down into Gran's rocker and watched the fire die to embers behind the closed glass doors of the safety inset. He didn't know how long he sat there, alternately talking to God and himself before Grandma Sheryl crept down the stairs to join him.

"What's the matter, Matt?" she asked him, laying her knobby hands on his shoulders.

"Just facing facts, Gran."

"And that would be?"

"That I don't deserve what I want."

She snorted, walked around and sat on the end of the coffee table. "Matthew, it's time you stopped blaming yourself for things that are not your fault."

"What do you mean?"

"Your mother did not leave because of you."

"I know that. She left because Dad wouldn't put up with her drinking."

"Your dad didn't die because of you, either, Matthew."

He sucked in his breath. This was much harder, a secret he'd never shared. "I—I was supposed to go with him that day."

"I know. You asked not to. He allowed you to go out with your friends. His decision, Matt, and one I've always been thankful for. You couldn't have helped him, and if you'd been on that tractor with him when it turned over, we might have lost you, too."

Matt bowed his head, feeling an odd relief. "The troubles you've had with the ranch…" he began.

"That's not your fault, either. I could have asked for help. I thought about it, but when I prayed, I felt God telling me to wait, to let Him work it out. That's not worked out so bad, has it?"

Matt shook his head. "No, not at all."

"The truth is, no one deserves what he wants, Matt, let alone all the good we receive. That's a matter of pure grace. At least you have sense enough and humility enough to know it, and that makes me very proud of the man you've become. Now just learn to accept gratefully the blessings God brings and go forward as best you can."

"Grandma," Matt said, "I'm so glad I came home."

"I am, too. It's made all the difference."

Matt grinned. "This has been the merriest Christmas ever."

"It's not over yet," she told him.

"No, ma'am," he said, getting up to kiss her cheek. "It is not."

Chapter Eight

Matt crept downstairs very early the next morning, surprised that he'd awakened before Amber, though in truth he hadn't really slept much at all. He had just hung the bow on the tree and switched on the tree lights when the phone rang. He rushed hopefully into the kitchen to answer it.

"Ender's Ranch."

"Matt?"

Nearly collapsing with relief, Matt shouted, "Marcus! Thank You, God!" He lowered his voice, grimacing. "Hope that didn't wake the girls."

"The girls?"

"Yeah, uh…Grandma Sheryl has a business partner named Neely Spence. She and her little sister, Amber, live here now."

"Oh. Well, I guess that makes this easier in a way, then."

"Makes what easier, Marcus?"

"Um, I know Grandma Sheryl's expecting me back down there, and I did say that I had no other plans, but… The thing is, I'm planning to stay here in Colorado, Matt."

"What do you mean you're staying in Colorado?"

"If the lady says yes, I'll be getting married."

Matt had to pull out a chair at the kitchen table and sit down.

"And here we were worried about you being stranded in the mountains," he said around a grin.

Marcus chuckled. "Seems like getting snowed in up here was the best thing that could've happened to me. I—I mean, I'm sorry to miss Christmas with you, but… I'm not entirely sure Grandma Sheryl didn't engineer this whole thing."

"How's that?"

"Matt, it's Sarah. I'm about to propose to Sarah."

"Sarah? Sarah, your high school sweetheart? That Sarah?"

"I know. She's the one who was selling the horses. Gran had to realize who she was when she sent me here. Right?"

Matthew pushed a hand over his face and then over the top of his head. "What matters is that you love her."

"I do."

"Then there will be other Christmases, all of us together."

"I'm glad to hear you say that."

"I mean it. I've missed my family. More than I'd realized."

"There's something else you should know, Matt. I wasn't sure I should tell you until just now."

"What's that?"

"It's about Mom."

Mom. Matthew steeled himself, waiting for the old

anger, the sense of abandonment. It came, but it didn't swoop in with the sharp talons of his angry youth. It edged in with the tired, shadowy sadness of maturity.

"What about her?"

"She contacted me."

Shock jolted Matt. "What did she say?"

"Wished me a merry Christmas, claimed she's gotten sober, hoped we're both well, asked if there was any chance we could connect."

Matt sat for several seconds, letting that news wash over him. "Wow. What did you tell her?"

"Nothing yet."

"What are you going to tell her?"

Marcus sighed. "Between you me, Matt, I've had a really, really difficult time forgiving her for just disappearing out of our lives like that. I mean, she abandoned us. There's no way to pretty that up. I just couldn't seem to get past it."

That surprised Matt. He'd never known his little brother harbored such resentment. Now, he, Matt, knew a thing or two about resentment. He'd majored in it all through his teen years. "I understand, Marcus, I do, but—"

"But," Marcus interrupted, "I think I'm ready to let it go now. I'm not saying we can pretend it never happened or be as close as we should've been, but maybe a little contact won't hurt. Might even help."

"Hey, Marcus," Matt asked after a moment, "have I ever told you that I'm really, really proud of you?"

The phone went dead silent for several seconds, then Marcus cleared his throat. "Right back at you," he said. "Now, get Grandma on the phone before we both embarrass ourselves."

Matt laughed, held the phone at arm's length and yelled, "Grandma! Your younger, uglier, less dependable grandson wants to wish you a merry Christmas!"

Sheryl came running into the room a few moments later, her glasses askew, her robe loosely belted. Neely and Amber followed on her heels. Given Amber's wide-eyed, eager manner, Matt assumed that she'd been awake for a while. Neely must have been keeping her in their room until the household roused.

Matt handed off the phone and went to slip his arm around Neely's waist. He desperately needed to touch her just then, to hold her if she'd allow it.

"Marcus?" Gran crowed. "I've been praying for you!"

"Is it really him?" Amber asked.

Matt nodded, smiling. "It's him."

Neely looked at him. "Everything okay?"

He folded her against him, his hand going to the back of her head. "Everything's great, sweetheart. Everything's just great."

She slid her arms around his waist and laid her head upon his shoulder, melting against him. A feeling of such gratitude hit him that it nearly took him to his knees. Fear swiftly followed it. What if this didn't mean what he hoped?

Sheryl hung up the phone and turned, clapping her hands. "Marcus is—"

"Great," Matt interrupted. Catching her eye, he gave his head a slight shake and mouthed the words, "Wait. Please." He couldn't bear to share Marcus's good news just now. They'd have time for that later. Matt had to settle some things first. With himself.

Gran looked to Neely then Amber and smiled broadly. "Marcus is great," she exclaimed. "I'm so relieved."

"When will he be here with those horses?" Neely asked.

"Not for a while," Gran answered, her gaze sliding away. "Got to get those roads open."

"But he's safe. That's what counts," Neely said helpfully.

"Exactly," Matt agreed, but suddenly he felt as if he had a hole in his stomach. He realized suddenly that this would be one of the most memorable Christmases ever, either the best or the worst, for both him and his brother. He sent up a silent prayer for his brother. He truly hoped that Marcus received the gift he most wanted. Was it too much to hope for that for himself, too?

While Sheryl set the percolator on the burner and Matt started a fresh fire, Neely and Amber began parceling out the gifts into piles, stacking Matt's on one end of the couch and Neely's on the other. Amber's pile, of course, was the biggest. Neely hadn't bought everything on her list but enough to make her happy for a good long while. She had to wait on the Santa gifts, though, and open those presents from Sheryl, Matt and Neely first, displaying appropriate gratitude, then letting the others open their packages before moving on to the big event.

Though literally quivering with anticipation, Amber behaved nicely, exclaiming over everything she received from family and friends, though most of it was clothing with a book or two thrown in for good measure. Neely went next, Sheryl insisting that they go by age, from youngest to eldest. Neely exclaimed over the framed watercolor painting that Amber had done for her—it really was quite lovely—and the crocheted sweater that

Sheryl had made. Neely tried not to be disappointed that she had no box from Matthew, though he'd said he'd try to find something more to her liking than Noble's gift. Perhaps he'd decided not to try to compete with Noble Wheaton. Didn't the big idiot know there was no competition?

As soon as her last gift had been displayed, Matt jumped right in, opening his gifts. He, too, received a framed painting from Amber and seemed very impressed that it actually looked like what it was supposed to, a horse. Sheryl's gift turned out to be a cowboy Bible with a hand-tooled leather cover. Matt handled it with great reverence and convincing gratitude. It made Neely's muffler, socks and knit gloves seem silly in comparison, but his thanks for those felt genuine and warm.

Sheryl cried over every single gift she received, from Amber's awkwardly painted linen hankie to Neely's selection of kitchen aprons and the boots that Matt had bought for her. The house plans, though, those both thrilled and troubled her.

"Matt, how can you afford this?"

"I'm not Noble Wheaton," he told her, "but I still have some winnings, and I can do a lot of the work myself. Besides, I don't expect to do it all at once. I'll get to it over time."

That last lifted Neely's spirits as much as Sheryl's. Time was what she dearly wanted with Matt. The more time he spent at the ranch, the better, so far as she was concerned. Who knew what might happen by next Christmas?

She finally gave Amber the go-ahead and watched as her baby sis tore through the pile of Santa toys, exclaiming more happily over each new gizmo than the one before until finally nothing remained but a pile of shredded paper and forlorn ribbon. Amber snagged her favorite items and bounded over to hug Neely's neck, proving once again that Santa had long since been relegated to the category of myth in Amber's mind.

"Looks like that's it," Neely said, reaching for one of the trash bags that Sheryl had brought into the room.

"Mmm, not quite," Matt said, looking pointedly at the tree. "I think Amber missed one."

Amber bounced up from the floor and hurried to the tree, quickly spying the big red bow tied there with a name tag hanging from it. She snatched it off the branch and looked at the tag. Her eyes grew large, and she suddenly thrust the bow at Neely.

"This is for you."

Neely looked at the name tag and the bow in her hands, but that's all it seemed to be, a bow and a name tag. "I don't understand."

Amber plucked the bow out of her hand and turned it over. That great big bow was tied to a ring with a very nice cushion-cut diamond mounted on it. She hadn't even figured it out yet when suddenly Matt knelt in front of her.

"I don't deserve you, Neely," he said softly, "but I do love you, and together I believe we could really make a great life together."

That's when she realized he was asking her to marry him.

She nearly bowled him over when she threw her arms around him. They wound up sitting on the coffee table in each other's arms.

Neely heard Amber crowing and Sheryl laughing,

but all she could think was, "What about the rodeo? Your hand is okay. You could compete again, but I'm not sure I can live that vagabond life again."

He shrugged. "That's not as important as what I have here with you. We can both compete again if we want to. Lots of couples do, and with Grandma here to help with Amber, we could work it out, plan a judicious calendar without living our lives on the road. But first we have to get the ranch on a more sound financial footing and build on a room. Or two. Unless you're against having kids of our own anytime soon."

Kids of their own. Neely started to laugh even as tears trickled from her eyes. "I love you," she declared just before she framed his handsome face with her hands and kissed him.

"Make that a room or three," Grandma Sheryl said, chortling.

"In that case," Matt said, "I've got one more bright idea."

"What's that?" Neely asked, clasping his hand.

"I've noticed that the old sign over the gate is missing."

"Rusted to pieces," Sheryl said. "I wanted to replace it, but with Neely coming on board, I didn't know what to call the place. Ender's didn't seem quite right anymore, but now that she's going to be an Ender, too, I guess it's okay. Still doesn't feel quite right, though. She saved this place as a Spence."

"I agree," Matt said, "so I was thinking." He looked to Neely. "We're building this place with my Blue and your Blaze, so why not…"

Neely grinned and looked to Sheryl to see if she'd get it.

"Blue Blazes Ranch," Sheryl announced. "That's what I call answered prayer."

"What do you think?" Matt asked Neely, leaning his forehead against hers as he untied the bow on her ring. "Partners forever?"

"Partners forever," she promised, letting him slide the diamond onto her finger. "In every way."

"And *now*," exclaimed Amber, "it's the merriest Christmas ever!"

"Or," Neely whispered against Matt's lips, "just the beginning."

"Yeah," he said, smiling gratefully and hugging her tight. "Let's go with that."

* * * * *

Dear Reader,

Sometimes we authors are blessed with a project that is much like going home again. This was just such a project for me. I grew up on a ranch outside of a small Oklahoma town very like Red Bluff, attending a small church where everyone knows everyone. It's a good life, where folks find ways to make livings that others wouldn't even think to consider.

As I write this, my dad's hat, boots and spurs adorn the fireplace in my living room and my grandmother's Bible sits on the shelf behind me. It wasn't all sweet memories, of course. Country living can be hard work! That's where I learned how well hard work pays off, however. Invaluable lessons.

I hope that, through Neely and Matt, I've conveyed something of that place and lifestyle, as well as the faith that underpins my life and work.

God bless,

Arlene James

COMING NEXT MONTH FROM
Love Inspired®

Available November 17, 2015

A RANGER FOR THE HOLIDAYS
Lone Star Cowboy League • by Allie Pleiter

Ranger Finn Brannigan wakes up in a hospital with no clue who he is. But this Christmas, with philanthropist Amelia Klondike by his side, he'll recover more than his memory—he'll find a love to last a lifetime.

AN AMISH NOEL
The Amish Bachelors • by Patricia Davids

Emma Swartzentruber has been content keeping house for her widowed father—until he announces she must marry. When former love Luke Bowman is hired to revitalize her family business for the holidays, could it be her chance at happily-ever-after?

GIFT-WRAPPED FAMILY
Family Ties • by Lois Richer

Widow Mia Granger is shocked to hear lawyer Caleb Grant say she owns a ranch—and has a stepdaughter. With his support, her bond with Lily grows and Mia realizes opening her heart could mean a new family this Christmas.

THE DOCTOR'S CHRISTMAS WISH
Village Green • by Renee Ryan

When Keely O'Toole becomes guardian to her seven-year-old cousin, she'll look next door to Dr. Ethan Scott for advice. Can the joy of the holidays and one little girl turn these dueling neighbors into husband and wife?

HOLIDAY HOMECOMING
The Donnelly Brothers • by Jean C. Gordon

Former television reporter Natalie Delacroix returns home to be with her family and take a break from her fast-paced life. Instead, she finds herself producing a Christmas Eve pageant and envisioning a future with her high school sweetheart, Pastor Connor Donnelly.

SECOND CHANCE CHRISTMAS
The Rancher's Daughters • by Pamela Tracy

Years ago, a painful tragedy made Elise Hubrecht run from her hometown—and her boyfriend, Cooper Smith. Now that she's back on her father's ranch, could this holiday season be Cooper's new chance with the girl who got away?

LOOK FOR THESE AND OTHER LOVE INSPIRED BOOKS WHEREVER BOOKS ARE SOLD, INCLUDING MOST BOOKSTORES, SUPERMARKETS, DISCOUNT STORES AND DRUGSTORES.

LICNM1115

REQUEST YOUR FREE BOOKS!

2 FREE INSPIRATIONAL NOVELS

PLUS 2 FREE MYSTERY GIFTS

Love Inspired®

YES! Please send me 2 FREE Love Inspired® novels and my 2 FREE mystery gifts (gifts are worth about $10). After receiving them, if I don't wish to receive any more books, I can return the shipping statement marked "cancel." If I don't cancel, I will receive 6 brand-new novels every month and be billed just $4.99 per book in the U.S. or $5.49 per book in Canada. That's a saving of at least 17% off the cover price. It's quite a bargain! Shipping and handling is just 50¢ per book in the U.S. and 75¢ per book in Canada.* I understand that accepting the 2 free books and gifts places me under no obligation to buy anything. I can always return a shipment and cancel at any time. Even if I never buy another book, the two free books and gifts are mine to keep forever.

105/305 IDN GH5P

Name _____ (PLEASE PRINT)

Address _____ Apt. #

City _____ State/Prov. _____ Zip/Postal Code

Signature (if under 18, a parent or guardian must sign)

Mail to the **Reader Service:**
IN U.S.A.: P.O. Box 1867, Buffalo, NY 14240-1867
IN CANADA: P.O. Box 609, Fort Erie, Ontario L2A 5X3

Are you a subscriber to Love Inspired® books and want to receive the larger-print edition?
Call 1-800-873-8635 or visit www.ReaderService.com.

* Terms and prices subject to change without notice. Prices do not include applicable taxes. Sales tax applicable in N.Y. Canadian residents will be charged applicable taxes. Offer not valid in Quebec. This offer is limited to one order per household. Not valid for current subscribers to Love Inspired books. All orders subject to credit approval. Credit or debit balances in a customer's account(s) may be offset by any other outstanding balance owed by or to the customer. Please allow 4 to 6 weeks for delivery. Offer available while quantities last.

Your Privacy—The Reader Service is committed to protecting your privacy. Our Privacy Policy is available online at www.ReaderService.com or upon request from the Reader Service.

We make a portion of our mailing list available to reputable third parties that offer products we believe may interest you. If you prefer that we not exchange your name with third parties, or if you wish to clarify or modify your communication preferences, please visit us at www.ReaderService.com/consumerschoice or write to us at Reader Service Preference Service, P.O. Box 9062, Buffalo, NY 14240-9062. Include your complete name and address.

LI15

Turn your love of reading into rewards you'll love with
Harlequin My Rewards

Join for FREE today at
www.HarlequinMyRewards.com

Earn **FREE BOOKS** of your choice.

Experience **EXCLUSIVE OFFERS** and contests.

Enjoy **BOOK RECOMMENDATIONS** selected just for you.

PLUS! Sign up now and get **500** points right away!

Earn
FREE
REWARDS
HarlequinMyRewards.com
Join!
Today!

MYR16R